P9-DCS-366

721 SECRETS

Keeping you up to date on all that goes on at Manhattan's most elite address!

Could it be that our resident lone wolf, Gage Lattimer, has found a mate? Sources say his new housekeeper has become a live-in...and *more* than a maid. Maybe that's why the workaholic is keeping regular hours. And just who is the mysterious Jane Elliott? Nobody can turn up anything on the secretive housekeeper. But she's apparently keeping Gage happy—with her skills. Cleaning skills, that is. But, really, Gage, she's the hired help. *Tsk-tsk*. Then again, Gage has had more than his share of troubles. Let's just say his reputation of late is less than sterling. Other rumors abound at 721. The latest is that the NYPD claim former resident Marie Endicott's death was not a suicide. Is it possible dangerous doings claimed the life of that sweet young thing in our own building? Only one thing's for certain: At 721 there's always a heap of secrets and scandals!

Dear Reader,

I was excited to be invited to write the final book in the PARK AVENUE SCANDALS continuity series. It was fun to be writing a story set in my native stomping grounds, New York City, as well as one featuring a British heroine (since I studied in the United Kingdom after college).

I hope you enjoy Jacinda and Gage's story. Jacinda is as daring as I've sometimes wished I was. And Gage—well, Gage can be remote but his outer shell is a cover for hidden depths. Watch Jacinda uncover the seductive man behind the mask!

Enjoy!

Anna

THE
BILLIONAIRE
IN
PENTHOUSE B

ANNA DePALO

Silhouette® *Desire*

Published by Silhouette Books

America's Publisher of Contemporary Romance

If you purchased this book without a cover you should be aware
that this book is stolen property. It was reported as "unsold and
destroyed" to the publisher, and neither the author nor the
publisher has received any payment for this "stripped book."

For my aunt and uncle, Corsignana and Michele Dagostino.

Special thanks and acknowledgment to Anna DePalo for her
contribution to the PARK AVENUE SCANDALS miniseries.

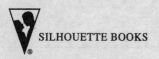

SILHOUETTE BOOKS

Recycling programs
for this product may
not exist in your area.

ISBN-13: 978-0-373-76909-4
ISBN-10:   0-373-76909-1

THE BILLIONAIRE IN PENTHOUSE B

Copyright © 2008 by Harlequin Books S.A.

All rights reserved. Except for use in any review, the reproduction
or utilization of this work in whole or in part in any form by any
electronic, mechanical or other means, now known or hereafter
invented, including xerography, photocopying and recording, or in
any information storage or retrieval system, is forbidden without
the written permission of the editorial office, Silhouette Books,
233 Broadway, New York, NY 10279 U.S.A.

This is a work of fiction. Names, characters, places and incidents are
either the product of the author's imagination or are used fictitiously, and
any resemblance to actual persons, living or dead, business establishments,
events or locales is entirely coincidental.

This edition published by arrangement with Harlequin Books S.A.

® and TM are trademarks of Harlequin Books S.A., used under license.
Trademarks indicated with ® are registered in the United States Patent
and Trademark Office, the Canadian Trade Marks Office and in other
countries.

Visit Silhouette Books at www.eHarlequin.com

Printed in U.S.A.

Books by Anna DePalo

Silhouette Desire

Having the Tycoon's Baby #1530
Under the Tycoon's Protection #1643
Tycoon Takes Revenge #1697
Cause for Scandal #1711
Captivated by the Tycoon #1775
An Improper Affair #1803
Millionaire's Wedding Revenge #1819
CEO's Marriage Seduction #1859
The Billionaire in Penthouse B #1909

ANNA DePALO

discovered she was a writer at heart when she realized most people don't walk around with a full cast of characters in their heads. She has lived in Italy and England, learned to speak French, graduated from Harvard, earned graduate degrees in political science and law, forgotten how to speak French and married her own dashing hero.

A former intellectual property attorney, Anna lives with her husband and son in New York City. Her books have consistently hit the Waldenbooks bestseller list and Nielsen BookScan's list of Top 100 bestselling romances. She has won a *Romantic Times BOOKreviews* Reviewers' Choice Award for Best First Series Romance and has been a finalist for the Golden Quill, Golden Leaf and Book Buyer's Best awards. Her books have been published in more than a dozen countries. Readers are invited to surf to www.desireauthors.com, and can also visit Anna at www.annadepalo.com.

Who's Who at 721 Park Avenue

6A: Marie Endicott—Now that her death has been determined as murder, how will 721's residents cope?

9B: Amanda Crawford—Not only was her affair with millionaire finance attorney Alexander Harper a secret...but so was her pregnancy!

9B: Julia Prentice—She and husband, Max Rolland, are anxiously awaiting the newest addition to their family!

12A: Vivian Vannick-Smythe—All evidence points to 721's longest-standing resident in the death of Marie Endicott.

12B: Prince Sebastian of Caspia—This royal couldn't be happier to make his ex-assistant, Tessa Banks, his new princess.

12C: Trent Tanford—The infamous playboy has tied the knot with Carrie Gray!

Penthouse A: Reed and Elizabeth Wellington—The Park Avenue powerhouse couple couldn't be happier.

Penthouse B: Gage Lattimer—The famed recluse has found his match in his new housekeeper...but is she who she says she is?

Prologue

5 months earlier

He had the lean, uncompromising face of a corporate warrior, the need to conquer stamped on his dark features.

But was he a killer?

Jacinda Endicott absorbed it all. The thick, dark brown hair, the intense brown eyes, and the granite jaw.

He wore a tux that outlined broad shoulders, and negligently held a champagne glass in one hand.

A dapper Cary Grant or George Clooney.

Still, he was unsmiling, nearly brooding even. He stared straight at the camera, a small but inescapable distance separating him from his companions. With his impressive height, he easily topped the couple on his right and the two men on his left.

Jacinda stared at the photo on her computer screen.

Gage Lattimer was enough to jump-start any woman's pulse, she thought, feeling an unwelcome kick in hers and frowning.

The billionaire venture capitalist and CEO of Blue Magus Investments kept a low public profile, but his air of quiet, self-assured power was nearly palpable.

He was the sort of man she could imagine her younger sister, Marie, being attracted to…before their affair had turned deadly.

Her heart squeezed.

It was hard for her to believe Marie was gone. Two weeks now. She kept waiting for the nightmare to end, but each morning, even before she opened her eyes, a feeling of dread coiled in her stomach.

She wondered whether things would ever be right again.

According to police, Marie had jumped from the roof of her swanky Park Avenue apartment building.

A suicide, the cops had said.

But Jacinda refused to believe her pretty and vivacious sister had taken her own life.

No suicide note had been found—and wasn't there almost always a note? Plus, the autopsy had found no drugs in her sister's system.

Jacinda shook her head. It didn't make sense.

Her sister had moved from London to New York right after graduation from the University of St Andrews, propelled by a sense of adventure. Marie had left her immediate family an ocean away, lured by the thrill and glamour of life in the orbit of *Sex and the City*.

In New York, her sister had landed a job as a commercial real estate broker, but had eventually left to start her own firm. With hard work and a sparkling personality, she'd soon netted several lucrative accounts.

And now Marie was dead. Cut down in the prime of life at twenty-five.

Because no matter what the police said, Jacinda knew in her heart her sister hadn't jumped. She'd been pushed.

But the question was, by whom? And why?

Jacinda's first clue had come by chance, when she'd flown to New York with her parents and brother right after they'd received a call from Detective Arnold McGray of the New York Police Department with news of Marie's shocking death.

At her sister's office, she'd met a broker that Marie had hired to work with her, and the woman had mentioned that Marie had been having an affair with a super-rich, powerful loner. Her sister had refused to name the man but had described him as tall and dark, with fathomless dark eyes and an adorable dimple.

Jacinda had latched onto the information. She'd also felt hurt—hurt that Marie hadn't confided in her about the relationship. But then she'd concluded Marie had probably assumed she'd disapprove of the man for some reason.

Of course she'd have disapproved if she'd had any inkling Marie's boyfriend had the potential for murderous violence.

Marie had been a free spirit and sometimes impetuous. She'd dated a guy with a nose ring in high school, and also a rocker with a mohawk.

Even so, Jacinda had never known her sister to choose a boyfriend as unwisely as she might have this last time.

Naturally, she'd gone to the police with the information her sister might have been having an affair. But the police had told her they needed more information—a lot more—to make the leap from a possible lover to a would-be murderer.

So, she'd combed through Marie's possessions... and come up empty-handed. As the police had already noted, there were no strange e-mails and no phone calls to an interesting number. Nothing.

The affair had either been a phantom or extremely clandestine, with a lover cunning enough to remain anonymous.

Desperate, she'd dug deeper, willing to look at anything. And that's when, in her sister's offices, she'd come across Marie's file on Blue Magus Investments.

Her sister had been trying to find new offices for the venture capital investment firm.

Scanning the file, her eyes had alighted on a name, Gage Lattimer, and her sister's neat, handwritten notations in the margin: *billionaire, well-connected* and *reclusive.*

Rich. Powerful. Loner. It had been enough.

Back at her hotel, she'd gone to Google and pulled up what little information existed on Gage Lattimer.

Now, Jacinda stared at her computer screen again. Physically, Gage Lattimer fit her sister's description, right down to how he towered over his companions. And though he wasn't smiling in the photo in front of her, she thought she could discern the indentation of a dimple.

He was thirty-five, divorced and eligible.

Through an online, people-finder service, she'd soon discovered Gage lived in a penthouse at 721 Park Avenue. Her sister's last address.

Bingo, she'd thought.

The coincidence had been too much.

For her, at least. The police were a different matter.

She knew she had to come up with more concrete evidence to interest the cops. They'd concluded Marie's death was a suicide, and they'd been dismissive of her claims of a secret affair.

They'd consider her batty now for accusing a powerful, quiet-living billionaire of murder.

Jacinda turned away from the computer screen and looked out her office window. But instead of seeing the rooftops and office buildings of Canary Wharf, London's newer financial district, she saw her reflection in the glass.

A classically pretty face stared back at her. Green eyes—cat's eyes, her mother called them—were fringed by thick, dark lashes, and balanced by an aquiline nose and a mouth with a full lower lip. Her long, curly brown hair was partly caught back by a crystal-studded barrette.

Marie had had similar features, but she'd been two inches shorter than Jacinda's own five-foot-eight.

If the police weren't interested in finding Marie's killer, then Jacinda would unearth the truth behind her sister's death herself. She owed it to Marie.

Her sister hadn't had a chance to embark on her life. She'd never get to travel the world. She'd never be a bridesmaid at Jacinda's wedding or meet any of Jacinda's children. She'd never get married and have children herself.

And, Jacinda thought, her sister's death two weeks ago had given a new immediacy to her own days. Suddenly, she wanted it all now—the husband, the kids, the full life.

What was she waiting for? Who knew how long she'd have on this earth?

She'd thought long and hard about what it would mean to take a leave of absence from her advertising executive position with the prestigious firm of Winter & Baker. But ultimately, with her plan taking shape in her mind, she'd known she had no choice.

She *had* to find Marie's killer. Otherwise, there'd be no resolution. Otherwise, she couldn't move forward with her own life.

Her family, of course, had been shattered by the news of Marie's death. Her parents and brother, Andrew, had been bursting with grief.

They'd been an upper-middle-class family and close-knit. Her parents' small business had generated enough of an income to send three children to well-known boarding schools.

But now Marie was gone.

Jacinda had gone with her parents and brother to retrieve Marie's body from the morgue and fly it back home, so her sister could be buried in the family plot outside London.

Unlike her, however, the rest of the family had reluctantly accepted the police's conclusion that Marie's death had been a suicide, if for no other reason than there was no evidence to the contrary.

But Jacinda hadn't been able to quell the feeling of unease inside her. She'd known Marie. Growing up, they'd been as close as any two sisters could be and, more than any other member of the family, she'd been privy to Marie's dreams and secrets.

There was no way her sister had committed suicide.

Jacinda swung away from the view outside—the office towers shimmering in London's July heat—and looked back at her computer screen.

Gage Lattimer. Was he the key to solving the crime?

Without allowing herself to hesitate, she picked up the phone and dialed the number for Marie's exclusive pre-War apartment building. Through directory assistance, she'd already tracked down the number for the reception desk in the main lobby.

When someone picked up, a man said, "721 Park Avenue."

The voice carried a distinct New York accent, and Jacinda reminded herself she'd have to disguise her own British accent if her plan was to have any chance of success.

She cleared her throat. "Hello. I'm calling on behalf of Gage Lattimer, one of your residents."

"Yes?" The man's voice held a hint of suspicion.

She assumed she was speaking with a doorman who manned the lobby of Marie's white-glove building.

Marie had moved to 721 Park Avenue only last year, and Jacinda had been there once, during her most recent trip to New York, after Marie's death.

At the time, she'd visited her sister's apartment alone and in disguise, because her plan had already started to form and she hadn't wanted to jeopardize it. She'd told her parents and brother that she didn't want to visit Marie's apartment with them because it was too painful to go there so soon after Marie's death.

"Mr. Lattimer will be returning to New York early and would like to contact his housekeeper so the penthouse is ready," she said, making her tone clipped and no-nonsense. "He's arriving with some guests."

"And you would be?"

She crossed her fingers. "His personal assistant."

"And you don't have Theresa's number yourself?"

"No," she responded coolly. "I'm new."

The man grumbled, "Just a minute."

Jacinda held her breath. She'd guessed the building staff at swanky 721 Park Avenue would know how to reach one of their residents' household help, if for no other reason than such contact information would be necessary in case of emergency.

And then, just like that, the man at the other end of the line was back, reciting Theresa's phone number.

"Thank you," she said before ending the call.

Without pausing for breath, not wanting to lose courage, she dialed the number she'd written down and crossed her fingers again.

She was done pretending to be Gage Lattimer's

personal assistant. But with any luck, she'd soon be playing his housekeeper—newly minted American domestic goddess Jane Elliott.

2 months earlier

Dropping his overcoat and briefcase onto a chair in the foyer, Gage walked into the vast, loft-like expanse that comprised the main living area of his modern duplex penthouse.

He'd only taken a couple of steps when he came to an abrupt halt—stopped in his tracks by the enticing vision before him.

A pert rear end, encased in low-rise jeans, moved alluringly back and forth and long, shapely legs tapered down to black wedge-heeled sandals.

His gut tightened.

He thought fleetingly that while the sandals were obviously a nod to New York City's warm July weather, at least her wedge-style heels could be considered a concession to practicality.

There sure as hell wasn't anything else practical about her, as far as he'd been able to ascertain.

She was bent over, seemingly feeling—dusting?— the underside of an end table near the fireplace.

A smile pulled at his lips before he suppressed it.

He cleared his throat.

"Find anything interesting down there?" he asked.

She straightened and whipped around, barely missing a solid glass lamp.

He watched as she placed a hand over her thumping heart and swallowed, her eyes wide.

Great, he thought. At least she was getting a dose of her own medicine. He'd been getting that pulse-racing sensation for months.

"I didn't know anyone else was in the apartment!" she exclaimed.

"I just got home."

They stared at each other, and Gage could almost hear the hum of sexual energy in the room.

Gorgeous, he thought for the umpteenth time.

She had the even, symmetrical features of a model, along with big green eyes and a mane of long, curly chestnut brown hair that had him wondering how it would look spread across his sheets.

She was above average in height, but her tall and willowy frame was audaciously balanced by round curves in all the right places.

His gut tightened again, and he wondered what she was doing cleaning apartments for a living. Even aspiring starlets who made their way to New York preferred to wait tables rather than push a vacuum.

It must be that she didn't have any connections and was too naive to exploit the marketability of her obvious assets.

She was a ripe little peach that had fallen into his lap. Except he wasn't picking from that tree anymore. A bitter divorce did that to a man.

Four months ago when his housekeeper, Theresa, had given him two weeks' notice, she'd recommended Jane Elliott for the job. Too busy to give it a second thought, and not wanting the hassle of contacting a housekeeping service and going through a series of mundane interviews, he'd agreed with the suggestion.

Theresa had been a good maid, but when she'd announced she was leaving to care for her sick mother, he'd had no doubt she could be replaced, especially with someone she recommended.

"You're usually not home this early," Jane said, cutting through the thick silence that had enveloped them.

He gave a brief nod. "I took the red-eye back from L.A. last night and went straight to the office." His lips quirked. "I'm short on sleep."

He could feel the strain around his eyes that came with sleep deprivation. In an unusual move, he'd left his Midtown office in the middle of the afternoon.

And yet despite having a demanding career, more often than was good for him he'd managed to come home to find Jane still puttering around the penthouse on one of the three days a week she was there.

He nodded behind her. "The underside of the table needs dusting?" he asked in a deadpan voice.

"Ah…"

The truth was she'd hardly been an excellent housekeeper. He'd invariably discover she'd missed something—forgetting to dust one of the rooms, for example, or not cleaning the hallway bath. It was one of the reasons why, as time went on, he'd offered her some overtime.

And yet, despite seemingly being unable to tell the difference between window cleaning spray and bathroom mold remover, his housekeeper knew her way around gourmet food and high-end entertaining.

During a cocktail party he'd hosted two months ago for some business associates, he'd noticed that she knew which cheese knife to lay out with what type of cheese and that she was familiar with imported wine labels. She'd asked probing questions of and offered knowledgeable suggestions to the caterer for the evening.

He'd liked listening to her husky singsong voice, letting it flow through him like fine, aged bourbon, even as he thought there was something about the woman he couldn't quite place.

Her accent wasn't a New Yorker's. Like a news broadcaster, she seemed to be from nowhere and everywhere.

She was a puzzle. And despite himself, he wanted to fit the pieces together. He wanted to get into her pants.

His lips firmed into a thin line. He'd been burned once, he reminded himself, and as a battle-scarred veteran of the divorce wars, he wasn't about to do something as asinine as getting himself ripped apart again over a pretty face.

Not that the face was merely pretty, he was forced to qualify. It rated as beautiful. Spectacular, even. Enough to make a guy not give a damn whether she remembered to dust his college baseball trophies.

"How did you say you and Theresa knew each other again?" he asked abruptly.

Her green eyes widened. "Theresa and my mother went to high school together."

"Right. I recall now that's what you said."

He stared at her. He couldn't help himself. She was so damn enticing, standing there in her typical work uniform of T-shirt and blue jeans. Today the T-shirt had an interesting green pattern that brought out the color of her eyes. It hugged high, full breasts that drew his attention as if he were a homing pigeon seeking to return to the nest.

He watched as she wet her lips and swallowed.

"I...I'm done in here." She turned to scoop up a disposable dust mitt lying on the couch. "And I'm nearly done cleaning the rest of the apartment. I'll be out of here soon."

After she scurried past him, he turned his head to watch her disappear through the arched entryway of the living room to the back of the apartment.

Damn. He was a masochist. Otherwise, why would he be torturing himself this way?

But who else would be willing to retain a so-so maid with a Gisele Bündchen body? Certainly not the society matrons with claws that prowled ritzy Park Avenue.

And what if Jane needed money?

Still, damningly, he had a disturbing attraction to his *maid*. He should give her a decent reference and dismiss her with a few weeks' severance. Before she really got under his skin.

Just then, Gage heard his cell phone ring and, with a grimace, he reached into the pocket of his pants.

He was reminded of the fact he was working on three hours' sleep, had finally gotten home and had had a chance to do little else but toss his overcoat on a chair and lust after his housekeeper.

A quick check of the screen identified the caller, and then he flipped open the phone. "Reed, good to hear from you."

"You won't be so happy to hear from me once you know why I'm calling," Reed responded.

Reed Wellington and his wife, Elizabeth, lived in the building's other penthouse apartment. The millionaire had been an investor in a couple of the venture capital deals Gage had put together. The mutually beneficial relationship had started when Reed's term on the building's co-op board had coincided with Gage's.

"What's up?" Gage asked, his voice sounding weary to his own ears.

"I'm guessing you didn't check your mail today."

"I just got home." Idly, he scanned the room. Jane usually retrieved his mail and placed it in a bin in his study.

"We're being investigated by the SEC."

He stopped, suddenly alert. *"What?"*

"You heard me."

"For what?" Gage set his jaw, ignoring the sting of sleeplessness at the edges of his eyes.

"The Ellias Technologies stock purchase."

Gage recalled the stock he'd recommended to Reed a few months back. He'd gotten a good vibe about Ellias—a high tech communications company— when he'd read about it in a trade publication. He'd run the name by his stock broker, who'd produced some stats for him to review and who'd agreed it was a good bet.

In short order, his faith had proved well placed. Only weeks after he and Reed had bought a sizable amount of stock, Ellias had landed a lucrative contract to provide the Department of Defense with radio systems.

Except now the Securities and Exchange Commission was sniffing around.

"We've been asked to voluntarily produce documents related to the stock purchase," Reed continued. "I'm sure your broker is being contacted."

"The SEC thinks we may have committed securities fraud?" Gage asked incredulously.

"I believe it's insider trading they're looking at, my friend."

Gage sobered. "You and I have known each other for a few years, Reed. You don't believe I recommended the stock to you based on non-public information I was tipped off to?"

"I trust what you've told me."

Gage felt some of the tension ebb from his shoulders. "Damn it. How much has each of us made off that stock? A hundred thousand or so, maybe? That's a drop in the bucket to people in our position, and it sure as hell isn't worth the headache of an SEC investigation!"

"I know, I know," Reed said, "but tell it to the feds."

"Damn it."

Reed made a sound of dry-humored acquiescence.

"Anyway, why the hell would they even think I acted on an insider tip?" Gage demanded.

"Good question," Reed responded, and then laughed shortly. "You'll never believe the coincidence."

"Spill."

"Guess who I just discovered sits on the Senate committee that green-lighted the Ellias contract?"

Gage's mind worked. He was acquainted with several public officials. Money talked, and with his kind of wealth, there were plenty of politicians who were happy to cozy up.

"Kendrick," Reed stated, not waiting for a response.

Gage cursed.

"Yup," Reed agreed.

Senator Michael Kendrick and his wife, Charmaine, had lived in their building until this past summer. Kendrick had even served a term on the building's co-op board—one that had overlapped with his and Reed's.

Gage recalled that, like a lot of other building residents, he had contributed to Kendrick's reelection campaign.

And now the SEC thought Kendrick had divulged some information about a government contract to him and Reed before it became public.

"It's worse than you think," Reed said. "Forget about the fact that Kendrick lived in the same building. I approached him about providing content for an Internet start-up that's an environmentally focused networking site."

"Damn," Gage said.

Reed's conversations with Kendrick could not have come at a worse time. They would make their connection to Kendrick look even more suspicious.

"I'm suspicious about the timing of this SEC investigation," Reed said.

"How so?"

"Remember the blackmail letter I received?"

Suddenly Gage made the same connection that Reed had. "You think the two are related?"

"Yup."

Reed had received a letter demanding he deposit ten million dollars in an untraceable Cayman Islands account, or else the world would learn the dirty secret of how the Wellingtons made their money.

Of course, the savvy investor had refused to pay. Someone of Reed Wellington III's Old Money connections and aristocratic bearing didn't get pushed around.

Gage would have relished explaining that face-to-face—or better yet, mano a mano—to the bastard behind the blackmail.

Reed had confided in him about the blackmail letter, but Gage had never fathomed the letter would come to this.

It was absurd. Beyond absurd. He had nothing to hide, and he knew Reed felt the same way. It was the reason the two of them had initially chalked up the blackmail letter as the work of some crackpot.

When you were in the billionaire's club, you got used to people trying to shake you down for cash. His ex-wife was a case in point, Gage thought, his lips twisting.

And then there were the drummed-up lawsuits, and even maybe a crazed blackmailer or two, as this case bore out.

It was one of the reasons he kept a fleet of lawyers on retainer.

Crap.

He felt the effects of fatigue and sleeplessness combining into a headache.

"Gage? Are you still with me?"

Reed's voice pulled him away from his racing thoughts.

"Yeah, I'm still here," he replied. "I need to call my broker and the lawyers. Once the SEC investigates, though, they'll discover there's no substance behind their suspicions."

When he signed off on his call with Reed, Gage swung around at a noise from the foyer, beyond the open archway of the living room.

He frowned, and a second later Jane peeked in, craning her neck beyond the limits of the archway.

"Sorry," she said, sounding breathless and looking guilty. "I was dusting a vase and accidentally sent it tottering."

Gage wondered fleetingly whether she'd been eavesdropping, and then dismissed the thought. What reason could she have to care about his personal financial affairs? If she were a criminally inclined housekeeper, she'd more likely be interested in stealing something from the penthouse.

But suddenly Jane's reappearance sent his thoughts traveling in a new direction.

Before he could debate the wisdom of the idea, he heard himself saying, "We need to discuss your cleaning schedule."

An alarmed look streaked across her face, and then she appeared fully in the archway. "Yes? Is there something wrong?"

Nothing but a case of runaway lust. Nothing that a good roll between the sheets wouldn't cure. "I'd like to offer you a live-in position."

Her eyes widened before she recovered. "Er—"

"This apartment comes equipped with maid's quarters, though they've rarely been used. Theresa stayed overnight only occasionally to clean up after a party."

"Oh."

"But I entertain more than usual in December." His lips twisted. "The holidays and all."

The fact was it was almost all business networking. Still, he felt compelled to entertain, even for business, in line with what end-of-the-year festivities called for.

She swallowed. "So the overnight position would be temporary?"

He surveyed her. Depends on how long it takes me to get over this crazy bout of lust.

"Why don't we see how things go?" he said smoothly. "I noticed during the cocktail party a few weeks ago that you did well pinch-hitting in the kitchen, and I have to admit even gourmet take-out gets boring after a while."

Her lips parted. "You want me to cook for you?"

He arched a brow. "Is that a problem? You've got me curious about your culinary skills."

She shook her head. "No. It's not a problem."

He was playing to her strengths. If she couldn't dust, at least she could cook. "It would only be occasionally. I often have dinner out with clients and business associates."

Her brow puckered. "I have a studio apartment—"

"You wouldn't need to give it up," he interjected. "You'd still have days off, though with the holiday season and entertaining, I'd prefer for it not to be on the weekends. How about Tuesdays and Wednesdays?"

Judging from her expression, she was wavering, as if trying to tally the pros and cons of his offer.

"Of course, you'd qualify for overtime pay," he said, sweetening the deal and testing his theory that she might be in need of cash. "Say, time and a half?"

"Your pay is already generous."

"I'm willing to pay for the best," he responded smoothly.

The best domestic help. The best cook. The best model-cum-housekeeper to waft around his penthouse driving him crazy.

"Well…" she hedged.

"Think about it."

She nodded. "Okay."

"Okay, you'll think about it, or okay, you accept?"

Their eyes met and held.

"Okay, I accept," she said.

"Great."

One

Present

She couldn't believe she was continuing this charade, Jacinda thought, as she deposited her overnight bag on the bed and set down a bag full of Christmas decorations next to it.

It was the beginning of December, and she'd been maintaining her pretense for five months.

Five long, wearying months that had gotten her no closer to discovering the truth about Marie's suspicious death.

The only bright spot was that her brother, Andrew, had informed her a couple of months ago that the police had come around to her way of thinking and were now treating Marie's death as suspicious.

But she didn't trust them to ferret out the truth. So, she'd continued to work hard to remember who she was pretending to be and not let her guard down.

It had been difficult to maintain her phony American accent, but fortunately she was a good mimic. A fake ID—procured through a hole-in-the-wall news dealer with a black market business on the side—had done much of the rest.

She glanced around the room. The maid's quarters were located on the lower level of the duplex penthouse, beyond the kitchen. They weren't opulent by any stretch of the imagination, but they were well-appointed with a full-size bed, a dresser and a night table, and an adjoining bath.

She'd gotten used to living here. On days like today, coming back after a day off, she'd cart along some clothes with her in an overnight bag, cycling through the wardrobe she kept at the small studio apartment she'd sublet on York Avenue and Eighty-second Street.

In fact, she thought, it was arguable which was bigger—her entire studio apartment, or the maid's quarters in Gage's 6,000-square-foot penthouse.

Her eyes alighted on the nearby dresser. The only thing the room lacked was a good dusting by a maid—except, she remembered, *she* was supposed to be the maid.

When she wasn't a sleuth.

Since she'd started working for Gage in July, she'd been stymied in her efforts to connect him to her sister's death. She'd discovered nothing going through his programmed phone numbers, rifling through desk drawers and scanning his mail.

Nothing except, she recalled, thinking back to October, she'd almost gotten caught snooping once when Gage had come home unexpectedly early and, in one of her more desperate moves, she'd been feeling along the underside of the end table next to the fireplace.

He'd taken a phone call immediately afterward that had made him frown mightily but, despite her best efforts, she hadn't been able to hear anything significant from the conversation.

Aside from that scanty bit of possibly tantalizing information, there'd been nothing. Absolutely nothing.

Instead, even with the help of a robot vacuum, she'd turned into the world's worst maid. It was hard to play amateur detective and still find time to scrub the sink.

She unzipped her bag and started putting her clothes in the dresser.

It was a miracle she'd convinced Gage's former housekeeper to quit. When she'd contacted Theresa by phone, she'd played dumb. She'd said she was looking for a unique situation because she was used to working with a moneyed and discerning clientele, which was the reason she wasn't going through a traditional employment agency to find a position.

Fortunately, her friend Penelope had been able to provide a sham reference, vouching for her as a fictitious former employer. Her closest friend from school days had married a rich and socially connected viscount and was happy to help by allowing her name to be dropped.

And as luck would have it, Theresa *had* been toying with the idea of moving on. In her early sixties, she was nearing retirement age and had a sick sister living north of the city for whom she wanted to provide care. She had been wavering, debating a move…until an opportunity had landed in her lap with Jacinda's phone call.

Of course, Jacinda admitted to herself, she'd embellished the truth a little bit. After some deft questioning, she'd led Theresa to believe her mother had attended the same Long Island high school as the housekeeper. For Gage, she had stretched the truth even further to make Theresa and the fictitional Barbara Elliott not only former high school classmates but also close friends.

It had all worked out, Jacinda recalled. She'd placed herself close enough to Gage to do some snooping, but she'd also been able to maintain some distance, coming into the penthouse three times a week, mostly when he'd been at work.

And then in October, Gage had stunned her by offering a live-in maid position. Caught off guard, and still feeling flustered by almost being caught snooping and then eavesdropping, she'd accepted Gage's offer.

Later, she'd justified her decision by focusing on how much more time she'd have to keep tabs on Gage and get the cleaning done.

But in the weeks since, she'd lain in her bed at night, awake and restless, knowing Gage slept feet away, his long, powerful body perhaps sliding between the russet-colored sheets she herself had placed on his sumptuous king-size bed earlier that day.

She'd tried telling herself her feelings were natural, caused by tension and alarm at being alone in the same apartment as a possible killer, vulnerable in her sleep.

But the truth was her feelings were simple and undeniable attraction.

Gage was a good-looking guy. Powerful, moneyed and well-built, he'd have been arm candy for any woman, if he wasn't so remote.

He was a typical lone wolf.

And rather than sensing criminality in him, she saw a wariness in his gaze that spoke of past hurt. It spoke to her and made her want to reach out to him as a kindred spirit. Because she'd suffered a personal loss herself. Marie.

She shook her head to clear it.

Her intuition was telling her Gage couldn't be a killer. But was lust leading her astray?

Done with emptying her overnight bag, she picked up her shopping bag full of Christmas decorations and headed to the living room. There, a boxed up Christmas tree and other assorted decorations awaited her attention. She'd had the building staff haul some of it out of Gage's storage unit in the basement yesterday. The rest she'd bought in the preceding days with some of the household money.

Frankly, she'd been surprised Gage owned as much of the mistletoe-and-holly stuff as he did. He struck her as a bit of the "Bah! Humbug!" type, actually. But she supposed when your net worth was ten figures, even a smidgen of holiday spirit amounted to a lot.

She sighed, her mind circling back to her earlier thoughts.

She'd been trying to uncover clues but the wrong ones kept coming her way.

For months, she'd been dusting Gage's baseball trophies—okay, when she remembered to dust his trophies—when what she needed to find was evidence of a more deadly hobby. Like hunting or collecting knives.

Instead, she'd compiled a dossier on Gage that would have made any would-be girlfriend weep with envy.

He housed three luxury cars—a Mercedes, a Lamborghini and a Porsche—in an underground garage, though he relied on a limo and driver most of the time.

He owned a getaway house in Bermuda, which was a couple of hours away from New York City on a direct flight with his private jet, which he kept parked at La Guardia and which he could fly himself with his pilot's license.

The Bermuda getaway was in addition to a house in London's fashionable Knightsbridge neighborhood, and a lodge in Vail, Colorado, where he liked to ski.

His Manhattan penthouse was a study in modern design—all glass and metal and hard edges, with cathedral ceilings, granite countertops and stainless steel appliances. Hand-recognition technology at the front door and touch-screen lighting controls throughout completed the picture.

His artwork was Abstract Expressionism, and she recognized works by Willem de Kooning and Jackson Pollock among those gracing his walls.

His business clothes, mostly custom-made, were from Davies and Son and Benson & Clegg, both long-established London clothiers.

He owned five Rolex watches, all housed in a glass-topped wooden case.

His toothpaste was Kiehl's, and he preferred to shave with an old-fashioned shaving brush.

The list went on and on.

She had all the details—except they weren't the details she'd come here looking for.

Who had killed her sister?

Truth be told, she hadn't even gotten a hint that Gage was interested in hitting on women. On the other hand, at a cocktail party he'd hosted weeks ago, she'd seen a couple of women send speculative looks his way.

And once or twice she'd caught him looking at *her* with hot eyes.

She shivered, remembering, and then focused on the task at hand.

She began to unwrap a glass ornament.

Gage had asked her to buy some because he liked to vary the decor for his annual December holiday party for friends and associates, donating some of the previous year's decorations to charity.

She wished she was going to be with her family back in London as the holidays approached.

Particularly this year. Their first without Marie.

But she'd set herself a task, and if Gage wasn't the killer, then who was? And who would help her find out?

It was the music that enveloped him first. The dulcet tones of Nat King Cole singing "The Christmas Song."

Next came the aroma of baking bread, wafting around him softly and getting his taste buds working in response.

Gage let the door click shut behind him as he walked into the penthouse, his brow furrowing.

He came to a stop at the archway to the loft-like living area, arrested by the sight of a huge Christmas tree standing sentry by the fireplace.

His tree, except this one was well on its way to being decorated with pink and gold ornaments.

He never did pink.

And that's when he realized *she* was humming.

He glanced over to the kitchen area and caught sight of Jane beyond the waist-high granite countertop, her back to him as she bent over the range of his chef's oven, unaware he'd come home.

Unbidden, the cozy scene had him making comparisons to holidays past.

Breaks from his New England boarding school… his parents, civil but distant and all too perfect…the house in Greenwich, Connecticut, decorated up to the chimney but emitting no real warmth.

Unlike the scene unfolding before him.

Damn it.

He set his briefcase down on a glass-and-chrome console table, and shed his overcoat.

"I'm home," he called out.

He felt ridiculous even as the words came out. This wasn't a scene from some TV sitcom of domestic bliss.

On the other hand, something like *Sex and the City* he could deal with. A vision flashed through his mind of Jane in sky-high heels and skimpy lingerie, bracing one leg on his bed and crooking her finger at him, beckoning.

He felt himself getting aroused, and cursed under his breath.

Just then, Jane swung away from the stove, her eyes going wide, a tea towel grasped in her hands.

Abruptly, he was called back from his fantasy.

It irked him that she always looked at him wide-eyed.

He jerked his head toward the tree. "Been busy?"

"Uh…yes. Yes, I have." She came around the kitchen counter, drying her hands and then setting down the towel.

"Do you…" She hesitated. "Do you like it?"

"It'll do."

Her continued wariness, and his damned unwanted attraction, made him brusque.

Her eyelids lowered, concealing the expression in her eyes. "Good."

He sized her up.

Today, she wore sensible black pants, a jade cotton top that stretched over her breasts, and what looked like ankle boots. Her hair, as usual, was caught back with a barrette.

He'd rather see her in silk, cashmere or satin. Her hair loose…

He reined in his wayward thoughts.

She bit her lip as they stood facing each other, several feet apart, squaring off as they often seemed to do.

She gave a nod over her shoulder. "It's potatoes au gratin, filet mignon and fresh bread. I was waiting for you to get home to sear the filets in a cast-iron pan."

She could sear his fantasies, he wanted to tell her.

Instead, he raised his brows. "Sear them in a cast-iron pan?"

He wasn't even aware he owned a cast-iron pan.

Her lips tilted upward at the corners. "It's a cooking trick I learned. Sear and broil."

"You said *filets,* plural."

She blinked. "Yes. They're on the small side and the specialty market on Lex was selling them in pairs—"

"Then you'll have to dine with me."

Her eyes went wide again, as if he'd suggested she strip off her clothes.

Actually, it was an enticing thought.

"Oh, I—"

"That's what they did in medieval times, you know."

"What?"

"Have a taster for the lord of the manor." He allowed a brief grin. "To make sure the food wasn't poisoned."

He pretended to look around. "And since there's no one else, I guess you'll have to fill in as the official food taster, as well as the cook and housekeeper."

She looked flustered. "Are you suggesting I'd poison you?"

"Or allow me to choke on a cloud of dust," he returned, one side of his mouth turning up.

He'd been teasing about the poison and the dust, but as he watched her redden, he sobered.

He needed to remember who he was and who she was. His maid, for Christ's sake.

"It'll be an opportunity for us to discuss the cocktail party I'm planning for the end of the week," he said.

And he hated dining alone. On the occasional night he was home for dinner, his thoughts had always drifted to Jane in the maid's quarters.

He'd wondered what she was doing and had had an unholy temptation to make her keep him company.

But his point about the cocktail party wasn't off the mark, either.

At least as far as household matters were concerned, their relationship had hit its stride.

In fact, he'd gotten used to leaving her notes around the apartment about what he wanted done. *Need shaving cream. We're out of coffee.*

Feel free to hop naked into my bed.

He stopped short and rewound. Wrong memory.

Still, despite his overactive imagination, their communications had taken on a familiar rhythm as she'd left him notes in return.

Leftovers in the fridge. I picked up your suit from the cleaners.

Almost like love notes. Except not.

They stared at each other.

He started forward, and she simultaneously stepped back.

He reached up to loosen the knot of his tie, and he watched her gaze fix on his actions.

As he moved past her, he murmured, "Smells delicious."

Looks delicious, too, he added silently. And I'm tired of dining alone.

She was out of her mind, Jacinda thought as she cut into her steak.

The tinkle of cutlery against china was the only sound against a background of low Christmas music.

The voice of Bing Crosby singing about a white Christmas drifted around them, since the penthouse was wired for surround sound.

She stole a look at Gage.

He looked freshly showered. While she'd finished making dinner, he'd obviously taken the opportunity to wash up and change into jeans and a crisp, light blue shirt.

If Gage had been Marie's lover, she could well understand what the attraction might have been for her sister.

He seemed like a guy she herself could date, Jacinda conceded. If circumstances had been different.

And while he'd been washing up, she'd worked herself into a mild panic at the thought of dining with him.

She'd contemplated setting the long table in the formal dining room with herself at one end and him at the other, but that had seemed too formal, despite his joke about an official food taster.

She hoped he hadn't read too much into her reaction

to his joke, though her heart had nearly jumped out of her chest when he'd mentioned *poison.*

Sure, if he'd harmed her sister, she'd love to pound him senseless—or at least see him brought to justice.

But she was having more and more doubts these days as to whether he was implicated in Marie's death. And Gage was right. They did have to discuss the details of the cocktail party.

As a result, she'd decided to set plates on the more informal table out in the loft-like living area visible from the kitchen—where they'd have a view of her unfinished handiwork on the Christmas tree and of the fire burning softly in the fireplace.

They sat at right angles to each other—him at one end of the table, and her to his immediate right.

She watched as he took a sip of his wine.

A 1990 California Merlot, if she remembered the wine label correctly.

When she'd first come across his impressive wine collection, she'd run her fingers over the bottles in the rack and thought that she'd have loved preparing meals to pair with some of the vintages she'd spotted.

Little had she known. Definitely a case of being careful what you wished for, since they now sat dining mostly in silence.

Except for the crackle of sexual energy in the air.

"I had my personal assistant send out the invites to the cocktail party a few weeks ago," Gage said, seemingly unaware of her nervousness. "We've got thirty yeses and five maybes."

She nodded. "I contacted a caterer. Someone new."

He raised his eyebrows.

"You'll like them," she went on in a rush, making her voice reassuring. "They were written up in *New York* magazine. Their lamb chops are superb."

"Sampling the goods?"

She felt herself flush. "I had a tasting when I toured their kitchen."

The truth was, she was sometimes at a loss as to what to do with herself during her time off. Besides worrying herself silly about this crazy scheme she'd embarked on, that is. And mourning her sister.

Gage's lips twitched. "I trust you as a food taster."

She wished she could say something.

He put the last bite of steak in his mouth and, after chewing thoughtfully, he said, "Why don't you dress for the occasion?"

She gaped at him. "Pardon me?"

He'd caught her so off guard, her British accent had leaked through. She hoped he hadn't noticed.

He studied her. "For the party."

"Oh." Well, that was better than what she'd initially thought, which was that he was criticizing what she was wearing tonight. How else was a housekeeper supposed to dress?

Still. "Is that a criticism?"

He gave her a veiled look. "No, a suggestion. It'll be a festive occasion. I thought you'd want to blend in."

"I'll be baking brie."

Instead of answering her directly, he nodded over to the tree. "You've been busy."

"But not nearly done," she admitted.

"I'll help."

Help. The last thing she needed was an enigmatic, too attractive gazillionaire hanging a wreath for her—even if he owned the mantel in question.

Through the apartment's hidden speakers came the voice of Josh Groban singing about being home for Christmas.

Ordinarily, she thought with a pang, she'd be at her parents' house for the holidays, decorating with Andrew and Marie. Instead, here she was with Gage.

She pushed back her seat, ready to start clearing the table now that they were finished with dinner. "It's my job."

They'd barely finished eating, but nervous energy made her restless.

She reached for his plate, but he moved it away, stalling her.

Their hands brushed, and they both froze.

Her eyes locked on his.

His face was uncompromising, but his eyes radiated dark heat.

She was reminded again he was a powerful man—physically fit and financially out of her league.

He could use his considerable wealth and influence to crush her if he ever found out what she was up to.

A tremor went through her.

"I'll help," he stated again. "I want to."

She sucked in a breath. "Okay."

A short time later, after they'd dealt with the dishes and she'd experienced the tabloid-worthy sight of a billionaire loading his own dishwasher, Jacinda found herself standing before the Christmas tree contemplating where to place her next ornament.

She watched as Gage bent forward to hang a pink Christmas ball, and let out an involuntary sigh.

He stopped and looked at her. "Something wrong?"

"Nothing."

When he looked unconvinced, she said reluctantly, "I was contemplating that spot."

He gestured in invitation. "Be my guest."

"You give in faster than either of my siblings."

The words were out of her mouth before she could give them a second thought.

"You grew up with siblings?"

"A brother and a sister."

"And you fought over decorating the tree?"

"Sometimes," she admitted. "But you don't show any signs of someone who had to fight for territory."

"That's correct. As far as siblings go."

If everything she'd read about him was true, Jacinda thought, Gage didn't concede an inch in business.

"No siblings?" she asked, though she knew the answer.

"None."

She nodded at the tree. "And you're a decorating amateur, too."

"Correct again." He looked at her archly. "Is that your way of saying I'm doing a bad job?"

"You're handling the ornaments gingerly," she said, sidestepping the issue. "As if you're not quite sure how to do this."

His lips quirked up at the edges. "And here I thought I was doing all right, given how many pink ornaments there are."

She felt herself flush.

Okay, she'd gone a little overboard in adding to his expensive and tasteful collection of Christmas decor.

But as a consequence, she'd seen again that he could be charmingly funny when he let his guard down.

"I couldn't help myself," she said apologetically. "I picked up a few pink ornaments."

"A few?"

"A minuscule portion of your net worth, I'm sure." The words popped out of her mouth before she could stop herself.

His lips twitched. "Do you have a thing for pink?"

Her chin came up, and she informed him with mock importance, "Pink is the new navy-blue."

He arched a brow. "You're kidding? I must not be reading enough *Cosmo*."

"Women are comfortable enough to wear pink these days," she said. "They don't feel compelled to dress like men. Pink is power. It's breast cancer awareness, among other things."

For a moment, she felt as if she were back at work, giving a presentation on market trends and successful advertising campaigns.

She wore pink in her other life as an ad executive. But he wasn't supposed to know about that existence.

"I thought a pink and gold theme would be refreshingly different."

Of course, it would, she thought. The rest of his

apartment was like the king of the jungle's lair. Black and glass and uncompromising male lines.

He looked at her bemusedly. "Right."

She stepped off her soap box. He was the boss, after all. "If you don't like it, I can always change…"

He looked at the tree, and then back at her. "No, I don't think so," he said blandly. "Let's try something different."

"*Refreshingly* different," she corrected him.

"Right. How could I forget?"

"So why don't you tell me why you're such a tree-decorating novice," she said despite herself.

"The staff always put up the tree in my parents' household," he admitted. "Everything was already done by the time I came down from boarding school."

His childhood didn't sound as if it had been made up of marshmallow memories.

"What boarding school did you attend?" she asked, though she knew the answer from her research.

"Choate."

"Oh, I know—"

She cut herself off. *I have an ad client who went there.* But she wasn't supposed to be too familiar with New England prep schools. Then again, at least she hadn't called them *public schools,* in the British way.

"You know…?" he prompted.

"It's in Massachusetts, isn't it?"

He nodded. "I sit on the board of directors."

Of course. "They must think highly of you."

She'd discovered he sat on many corporate boards as a venture capitalist with money sunk into numerous and far-flung enterprises. He was always flying off to one place or another.

"School was sometimes more family than family," he said.

Nope, not a single marshmallow memory, it sounded like. "I'm sorry."

"Don't be," he said. "It's just a fact. My parents weren't bad parents. They were just older, and they insisted on a formality that was true to their generation."

She glanced back at the tree. Perhaps she should have maneuvered to dine with him weeks ago instead of hiding out in the maid's quarters. She felt as if she was finally noticing the seams in the facade of Gage Lattimer.

She cleared her throat as she hung up her ornament in the spot he'd conceded to her. "Are your parents still living?"

"Yes. They retired to a chalet in Switzerland five years ago." After a moment, he hung up his ornament in a new spot.

She longed to ask where in Switzerland, because she'd gone skiing with friends in the Alps a couple of times, but she held her tongue.

Perhaps it was the Christmas music, or maybe it was being far from home at the holidays, but she had to battle the urge to reach out to him.

She took a deep breath, deciding to take the bull by the horns. She *had* to ask him about Marie's death.

She'd run out of options, and her snooping hadn't gotten her anywhere. She was desperate.

"Have you enjoyed working here?" he asked abruptly, surprising her.

She clamped her mouth shut, and stared at him.

He looked almost as surprised as she did by the question. And almost as uncomfortable, too.

She picked up another ornament from the box she'd set down on a nearby table. "Wouldn't anyone enjoy living in an enormous penthouse in the heart of Manhattan?" she said flippantly, before knitting her brows and deliberately lowering her voice. "Of course, there have been some strange happenings."

He stilled. "Such as?"

She forced herself to look at him directly. "I heard there was an apparent suicide a few months ago." She paused. "A woman jumped from the roof?"

He frowned. "Where did you hear that?"

"Oh, you know," she said, waving the hand with the ornament. "One of your neighbors, I guess, was talking in the elevator."

His expression smoothed. "Yes, it was tragic."

"Did you know her?" *Did you sleep with her?*

Please God, let it not be him. Suddenly, it was crucial to her that Gage not be the one.

"She was my real estate broker."

She forced herself to play it cool. "Oh?" She looked around. "I thought you'd lived here for a number of years."

"I have. I didn't hire her to find me an apartment, but for new offices for Blue Magus."

"And that was your only connection to Marie Endicott? Was that her name?"

"You sure have a lot of questions," he said, his tone half-teasing.

She shrugged. "Simply curious."

He hung up the ornament he was holding, and then turned back to her. "Yes, she was my broker. Nothing more. But after she died, I temporarily pushed back finding new offices for my firm for a number of reasons."

"Oh." Relief washed through her.

"Why are you so curious, Jane?" Gage added in a low voice. "Do you want to know if I'm involved with someone?"

She hated to admit she did. "Are you?"

"No."

You have me hypnotized…

"Are you?" he asked.

…so hungry for you I'm desperate for relief.

"No."

He moved closer, and she forgot to breathe as he picked up a strand of her hair and toyed with it.

The air hummed as her lips parted and her eyes lowered to his mouth.

He had chiseled lips. And yet they looked soft, as if they could give and receive infinite pleasure.

"Jane."

She sucked in a breath…and then a second later, it hit her.

Jane. Not Jacinda. *Jane.*

What was she doing? She was living a lie.

She stepped back. "I—I have a phone call to make."

It was a lame excuse, and she could see from the expression in his eyes that he saw right through her.

She turned and bent to drop her ornament into its box.

And then she fled, driven by conflicting emotions that threatened to engulf her.

She had arrived in New York wanting to hate Gage Lattimer. But since then she'd had doubts about his guilt. And the whole matter had been clouded by her physical attraction to him.

If Gage wasn't responsible for her sister's death, maybe he could help her—if she could keep her attraction in check.

Except there was no way she could risk telling him how she'd tricked him, was there?

Two

"Andrew!" Jacinda said. "H-how are you?"

Jacinda juggled her packages as she trudged along East Seventy-third Street.

When her cell phone had rung and she'd recognized the number as her brother's, she'd felt compelled to pick up.

No use letting her family worry about her any more than they already did. They had enough on their plates. Jacinda knew her mother was still seeing a grief counselor.

"I could ask the same thing about you," Andrew responded. "How are you doing?"

"I'm fine."

She'd maintained the pretense for her family that

she was in New York taking a sort of break, winding up Marie's affairs and giving herself some breathing room from work to come to terms with Marie's death in her own way.

Jacinda hurried across the street as a cab honked at her. When she reached the opposite curb, she looked up at the sky. It was an overcast and chilly day. It reminded her of London weather, actually.

"Have you heard anything more from the police?" she said into the phone, in part to deflect attention from the dangerous topic of what exactly she was doing in New York.

She relied on her brother to keep her up to date on the police investigation. She didn't want to call the police herself from a local number and raise questions about her presence on this side of the Atlantic. And she most assuredly did not want the police calling her on her cell when Gage might be around.

"It was the reason I gave you a ring, actually," Andrew responded.

"Oh?" She perked up as she rounded the corner onto Park Avenue. The trees along the avenue's center divider were decked out with holiday lights.

"I spoke to the detective on the case this morning," Andrew said. "Detective McGray."

Jacinda remembered that Detective Arnold McGray had made the first contact with her family in the immediate aftermath of Marie's death, when police had ruled it a suicide. But because she was already hatching her plan to go undercover, she'd taken care not to meet the man in person.

"And?" Jacinda asked. "Don't keep me in suspense."

"It seems there have been a number of attempts to blackmail residents at 721 Park Avenue."

"What?"

"You heard me. Some residents have gotten demands for a million dollars or more. And the police think the blackmailer may also be responsible for Marie's death."

"How long have the police had this theory?" she asked, her voice sharpening. "Surely they didn't just discover that a number of people were being black-mailed."

"They put the blackmail schemes together with Marie's death a while ago," Andrew replied, "but they only saw fit to mention it to me now."

To Jacinda, it was yet another sign the police were being slow and desultory in their investigation of Marie's death.

Still, she forced herself to keep walking despite feeling weak-kneed. "Do they have any idea who might be behind it all?"

"No, except since all the crimes involve residents of 721 Park Avenue, they think it's someone who's familiar with the building. Also, there was no one signed in on the doorman's visitors' log from the night of Marie's death."

Jacinda squeezed her eyes shut. This whole thing was getting bigger than she could manage. Their murderer might also be a blackmailer.

And then she had a sinking feeling in her stomach. *Gage.*

This could be the crucial bit of information that

ruled him out as a suspect—which meant she'd been barking up the wrong tree these past months.

A billionaire didn't have any need to blackmail people for a paltry million.

What was she going to do?

If only she could recruit Gage, she thought, her mind racing, not really thinking rationally.

If Gage was innocent, then he could be a valuable ally in her quest to find the perpetrator.

Gage had the money and the resources. The power and the influence.

Power.

Actually, it had been Gage's potent masculine allure that had made her feel most unsafe these past several months, when she'd found herself more and more doubting Gage could have been involved in Marie's death.

Jacinda remembered their encounter of a few nights ago in front of the Christmas tree, before Gage had thankfully left for a few days on a business trip.

Gage's gaze had rested on her, and she'd fled from the room, feeling a heat that had had nothing to do with the crackling fire.

But their sexual attraction only added complications to an already complex brew.

She'd tricked him. She'd approached him under false pretenses, masquerading as a maid with a contrived American accent and a phony background.

Something told her that a prominent and savvy guy like Gage wouldn't take well to discovering he'd been duped.

She winced.

"Jacinda? Are you there?"

"Yes." She glanced up at the green street sign at the corner. She was nearing 721 Park Avenue. "But I must ring off. I'm at my destination."

"Okay, but keep in touch," her brother responded. "And, Jacinda?"

"Yes?"

"Take care."

If only her brother knew. "I will."

After ending her call, Jacinda automatically stopped by Park Café, an upscale coffee shop at the corner of Gage's building. She did a quick scan of the shop, and noticing nothing significant, sighed and went to the counter to place her order.

When she'd first arrived in New York, she'd taken to dropping into Park Café as a way of observing Marie's neighbors. But none of them had aroused her suspicions.

She'd also struck up a conversation with the principal barista, who had recollected that Marie would stop by for a latte but hadn't recalled seeing her with anyone who looked like a date.

Even so, these days Jacinda continued to drop into the café sometimes before she went to work, hoping against hope that something interesting would turn up.

Today in particular, she acknowledged, she'd walked in hoping to win the proverbial lottery to get her out of her current mess. If only she could get a clue that led to Marie's killer, she could go to the police and then immediately leave the city before Gage was any the wiser about her deception.

But today wasn't going to be her lucky day, as a quick search of the nearly empty shop had revealed.

At the counter, Jacinda greeted the barista and placed an order for hot chocolate. She needed a comfort drink after the news that Andrew had imparted.

She realized resignedly that she was committed to a course of deception with a man who was likely innocent while she continued to search for Marie's killer. Her position as Gage's maid gave her a reason to hang around 721 Park Avenue without arousing suspicion, and that was even more crucial now that the police believed Marie's death was perpetrated by a building insider.

After collecting her hot chocolate, Jacinda exited the café and headed toward the entrance of 721 Park Avenue.

She acknowledged the doorman, Henry Brown, and then stepped inside the building.

Immediately, she was met by yapping dogs, causing her nearly to spill her drink.

After taking a moment to compose herself, she said, "Hello, Mrs. Vannick-Smythe."

She'd never warmed to the building's grande dame, and certainly not to the woman's shih tzus, who seemed to bark at everyone.

Mrs. Vannick-Smythe gave her the ghost of a smile, before commanding, "Louis, Neiman, down."

After a moment, the twin white shih tzus ceased their barking and sat back on their haunches.

Jacinda smiled gratefully at the older woman, but in return, the building's grande dame simply stared at her piercingly.

As usual, Mrs. Vannick-Smythe was dressed in a tailored suit, her silver hair cut in a sleek bob that accentuated her pale blue eyes.

If Jacinda had to hazard a guess, she'd say today's suit—a cranberry wool number with gold buttons— was either Chanel or St. John.

Jacinda shifted from one leg to the other. Mrs. Vannick-Smythe and her dogs always made her feel as if they could scent an imposter in their midst.

"Well, I'd better get to work," Jacinda muttered, and then marched to the elevator and stabbed the Up button.

Fortunately, the elevator arrived just moments later, and she stepped inside.

A man stepped into the elevator with her before the doors closed.

Jacinda groaned inwardly as she got a look at him.

Sebastian Stone, otherwise known as Prince Sebastian of Caspia. Her brother's old preparatory school classmate.

He remained tall, dark and good-looking, with strong patrician features.

She'd known Sebastian Stone was living in this building—Andrew had mentioned it after Marie had died. But Jacinda had made it her job to find out which apartment and what he looked like these days, so she could avoid him and any questions about what she was doing at 721 Park Avenue.

And fortunately, until today, she'd managed to avoid running into him. She knew he'd been out of the country for significant periods because she'd gotten chummy with his apartment sitter, Carrie Gray, who was now married to another resident, media scion and former playboy Trent Tanford in 12C.

But it looked as if her luck where Prince Sebastian was concerned had come to an end.

She just hoped now that Andrew hadn't shared any photos of her with Sebastian whenever they'd recently been in touch.

When Prince Sebastian looked at her quizzically, she tensed.

"Pardon me if I sound rude," he said, his voice betraying the hint of an accent, "but do I know you?"

"Ah…"

The man stuck out his hand. "Sebastian Stone."

Jacinda gulped and stalled.

Sebastian looked puzzled, but continued to hold out his hand.

"I'm not a resident here," she said in her best American accent, avoiding his eyes. "I'm the cleaning lady for Penthouse B."

She hoped she sounded suitably deferential and, more importantly, inconsequential.

"Oh?" Slowly, Prince Sebastian withdrew his hand. "I could swear—"

"You've probably noticed me around the building before," she muttered.

Out of the corner of her eyes, she watched him nod.

"That must be it," he said, though he sounded far from convinced.

When the elevator doors opened on the twelfth floor, and Prince Sebastian blessedly moved forward, she exhaled.

"Have a nice day," he said.

"Yes, you, too," she managed, stabbing the elevator's Door Close button as he stepped out.

Come on, come on.

When the doors closed, she sighed with relief.

Running into Prince Sebastian seemed par for the course. Today was *not* her day. First the call with Andrew, then Vivian Vannick-Smythe and now running into Prince Sebastian.

Her situation was getting more and more precarious—despite her glib assurances to Andrew.

What else could go wrong?

Then she remembered Gage's cocktail party was that night.

"Happy holidays!"

Gage smiled as he leaned down for a kiss on the cheek from Elizabeth Wellington.

"Right on time," he said, knowing the cocktail party behind him was getting under way and the musicians had just struck up another holiday tune.

"We brought a vintage Cabernet with us," Reed said, holding the bottle out to him as he stepped into the apartment. "Courtesy of the Wellington wine cellar, of course."

"Thanks." Gage gave Reed a meaningful look full of humor. "I'll put it in the pantry. I'm sure Jane will be able to use it for cooking one dish or another."

"Doesn't your own wine serve that purpose?" Reed parried. "I've been trying to elevate your tastes."

Elizabeth shook her head with mock resignation.

"Stop it, you two. It's the season for goodwill toward all men. Let's make merry."

"Ho, ho, ho?" Reed put in.

Ignoring her husband's dry humor, Elizabeth turned to Gage. "Thanks for inviting us."

Gage smiled. "I'm glad you could make it, since having a new baby is a lot of work."

"Don't be silly," Elizabeth replied. "You're just across the hall from us, after all!"

"The truth is," Reed joked, "I had to tear her away from Lucas, even though he was in good hands with the babysitter."

Elizabeth looked at her husband fondly.

Gage knew the Wellingtons were in the process of adopting Elizabeth's orphaned eleven-month-old nephew, Lucas. They carried a new aura of contentedness about them, particularly Elizabeth, not only because of Lucas but because she had recently announced her pregnancy.

Gage stepped aside. "Come on in. Some of our neighbors are already here."

"Don't tell me you invited Vivian Vannick-Smythe?" Elizabeth murmured as she passed him.

A smile played at Gage's lips. "Had to," he murmured back. "But don't worry—her dogs are at home."

"Thank goodness."

Gage looked up and noticed Jane approaching them.

His eyes swept over her hungrily, but he was quick to veil his expression.

She was wearing a sleeveless black cocktail dress that skimmed her lush curves. Her hair was swept up in a loose style, and black pumps revealed legs that could make a man whimper.

He felt his body tighten.

He was pleased she'd taken his suggestion to dress up a little for the evening. At least, he flattered himself that she'd dressed with him in mind.

Ever since their near-kiss days ago, before his latest business trip to Chicago, he hadn't been able to get her out of his mind.

In fact, he'd been suffering the tortures of the damned.

How does a guy go about seducing his house-keeper? It was a ridiculous question, really. It made him feel like some latter-day Regency lord tempted to take advantage of the backstairs maid.

On the other hand, he rationalized, they were both adults, and why should he give a damn that she was his maid?

After their moment in front of the Christmas tree, he knew their attraction was mutual. He knew he hadn't mistaken the light of awareness in her eyes.

He should just seduce her and be done with it. Get her out of his system, and move on.

He'd get another housekeeper. And she— Well, she could go on to conquer the billboards and catwalks of New York, if she wanted to. He'd help her.

Ever since his divorce, women had come and gone, but with everyone, Gage had been clear from the beginning that all he could offer was a no-strings affair. He wasn't one to lose his head or his heart—not anymore.

Of course, he hadn't dated anyone in over six months. Since before Jane arrived, now that he thought about it.

And after seeing the way Jane was dressed tonight, Gage thought that his seduction idea had even more appeal.

When Jane reached them, she looked from Reed to Elizabeth, a smile curving her lips. "Would either of you like a drink?" She nodded behind her at the two bartenders who had been hired for the evening. "I'd be happy to fetch you both something."

Elizabeth smiled with genuine warmth. "Hello again, Jane. Did you have a chance to visit the new specialty market on Second Avenue that I suggested to you?"

"I'm glad you did suggest it, actually," Jane responded. "Thanks to my trip, I made my first soufflé in ages."

Elizabeth slipped her arm through Jane's. "You have to tell me all about it." She looked up at Gage over her shoulder. "You don't mind if I steal away your housekeeper, do you, Gage?"

"Not at all."

Gage watched the two women move off.

He was called back from his thoughts, however, when he realized Reed had said something.

"What?" he asked.

Reed chuckled. "You didn't even hear what I said."

"Now that you mention it…"

Reed tossed him a droll look. "I said, she looks great, doesn't she? Those legs?"

Gage's brows pulled together. "Aren't you happily married?"

Reed laughed again. "It didn't even occur to you I might be referring to my wife, did it?"

Damn. "Forget it, Wellington."

The last thing he needed, Gage thought, was to be giving the impression that he wanted to hit on his housekeeper.

Even if it was true.

Reed seemed willing to change the subject, because he sobered a little. "Well, at least we don't have that insider trading investigation by the SEC to worry about anymore."

Gage nodded. "You got that right."

The Securities and Exchange Commission investigation back in October had unearthed an e-mail that had implicated one of Senator Kendrick's aides and two of the senator's associates in insider trading.

There had been no evidence tying Gage and Reed, to anything, so the SEC had dropped them from its investigation.

Good for him and Reed, Gage thought, bad for Senator Kendrick.

Senator Kendrick had declined his invitation to tonight's party, and Gage supposed it was because the man currently had the scent of scandal on his hands.

Gage watched as Reed's lips twitched again, and he looked at the other man inquiringly.

"And, one more thing," Reed said. "Don't worry about Elizabeth poaching your housekeeper."

"Why would I worry about a thing like that?"

Reed shrugged with nonchalance, but Gage wasn't fooled.

"From the way you were looking at Jane," Reed

said, "someone might think more was going on between you than stain removal and dust busting."

"Getting it on with my housekeeper?" Gage said in a tone of deliberately exaggerated disbelief, this time ready for the gibe. "I don't think so."

His fantasies were another matter, however.

"The way she's dressed, she looks more like a hostess than an employee," Reed observed.

"I suggested she dress up for the evening," Gage replied evenly. "She deserves most of the credit for tonight's success. Why shouldn't she enjoy it?"

Reed just raised his eyebrows before he sauntered off. "I think I'll go check on what sorry excuses for wine you're serving tonight."

"Do that."

As Reed walked away, Gage looked down at the wine bottle in his hand, and his lips twisted wryly.

A 1996 Cabernet. Trust Reed to make a statement.

He decided to walk it over to the kitchen, and soon thereafter, other past and present residents of 721 Park Avenue arrived at his door.

Trent Tanford and his wife, Carrie, came in the door steps ahead of Amanda Crawford and her fiancé, Alexander Harper.

In short order, his newly arrived guests were mingling with Vivian Vannick-Smythe and others in front of the Christmas tree, while the hired wait staff walked among them with hors d'oeuvres.

And as the evening progressed, Gage observed that Jane had apparently made friends when he hadn't been looking.

Of course, his neighbors had come to his parties in the past. But this year, since Jane seemed to be on friendly terms with nearly everyone, it seemed more like a gathering of friends.

Gage's gaze settled on Jane as she encouraged Steve Floyd, one of his business clients, to sample the smoked ham and other dishes that had been set out on a nearby table.

Steve appeared completely charmed and, in no time, seemed to be flirting with Jane.

Gage's eyes narrowed as he experienced a kick in the gut. If he hadn't known Jane would end the evening at his place, he'd have been tempted to go over and break up Steve's little tête-à-tête.

He was still tempted. But he didn't need to give Reed any more ammunition that he had it bad for his housekeeper.

But, Jane had certainly infiltrated his life, Gage reflected. Even his clients were falling under her spell.

The question was, how long would she stay out of his bed?

Three

As the evening wore on for Gage's holiday cocktail party, Jacinda found herself standing next to Gage among a group of past and present 721 Park Avenue residents.

She thought the party was going exceedingly well. And Gage seemed to be enjoying himself, too. Well, except for when she'd caught him frowning while she'd been speaking to Steve Floyd.

Glancing around her now, she noted that Elizabeth and Reed Wellington were standing in an informal little circle with her and Gage, as well as Carrie and Trent Tanford, and Amanda Crawford and Alexander Harper.

Jacinda had made it her business to get friendly with as many people as possible at 721 Park Avenue— except for Sebastian Stone—in the hopes she'd pick up some clue about her sister. Unfortunately, she'd gotten nowhere.

Everyone had concurred that Marie's death had been tragic. Not surprisingly, those of her neighbors who had known Marie better had remembered her as an upbeat, energetic young woman. But when Jacinda had suggested that perhaps there was a boy-friend or significant other who was mourning Marie's death, no one could remember seeing her with a regular date.

Jacinda hadn't even gotten any good information from the doormen—not even the most regular of them, Henry Brown, who'd been rather tight-lipped about the whole issue of Marie's death, as if gossiping went against his porter's code of discretion.

"Are you expecting anybody else we know to show tonight?" Trent Tanford asked, breaking into her thoughts.

Gage shook his head at Trent. "Max and Julia Rolland had to decline my invitation because Julia is due to give birth any day. They're holed up at home."

"Julia can't wait for the baby to be born," Amanda chimed in. "I spoke with her this morning and she swears all she can do is waddle like a penguin at this point."

Jacinda knew Julia and Amanda had been room-mates in Apt. 9B until Julia had married in July—shortly after Jacinda's own arrival in New York—and moved out of the apartment.

And then last month, Jacinda had noticed Amanda sporting an engagement ring. When she'd inquired, Amanda had confessed to being engaged.

"I invited Senator Kendrick," Gage added, "but he'll also be a no show."

Jacinda was familiar with the name. She recalled Marie had been volunteering with Senator Michael Kendrick's reelection campaign. She'd seen flyers in her sister's apartment and office.

"I didn't know you were friendly with the senator," she commented to Gage.

Gage glanced at her, and then leaned in to add for her ears only, "I don't socialize with him, but I added him to the guest list for tonight to keep up an important connection."

Jacinda nodded, feeling a tingle down her spine at Gage's nearness.

"What about Prince Sebastian and Tessa Banks?" Carrie asked.

"They also sent their regrets," Gage replied. "They're flying out to Caspia tonight for a few days to continue arranging their upcoming wedding. Because of Caspian business, the prince and his bride have been forced to delay the ceremony till spring."

Jacinda knew from the newspapers that society tongues had wagged when it had been announced in September that the Caspian heir to the throne would be marrying his American personal assistant.

"Speaking of weddings," Trent said, giving his wife a smile, "I hope you've all received mine and Carrie's wedding invite for New Year's Eve. We're tying the knot again—this time with a church wedding."

"Twice in one year?" Alex Harper joked. "You've got nerves of steel, man."

"We're doing it right this time," Carrie put in as Trent gave her a quick squeeze. "It'll be a big evening wedding, instead of a more impromptu affair."

"Congratulations," Jacinda murmured.

The *New York Post* had belatedly published photos in early August of Trent Tanford nuzzling and holding hands with her sister at hip Manhattan nightspot Beatrice Inn. There'd been dark speculation by the media and even the police.

But Jacinda had known they'd been barking up the wrong tree. Marie had confided to her that she'd gone out a couple of times with the renowned playboy when she'd first moved into 721 Park Avenue, but nothing had come of the dates. And when Jacinda had combed through her sister's possessions after her death, she'd been unable to locate any evidence that Marie had continued her relationship with Trent.

Instead, Jacinda believed what Marie's coworker had told her—that Marie had been seeing a super-rich, powerful loner whom she refused to name.

Moreover, Trent Tanford wasn't a loner. He'd been a world-class playboy for whom women came and went until his marriage in August to Carrie, who'd been apartment sitting for Prince Sebastian.

Marie had in all likelihood been nothing more than one in a long series of women with whom Trent had amused himself.

And on top of it all, Jacinda had seen evidence of Trent's playboy ways herself when she'd begun working at 721 Park Avenue. She'd run into Trent more than once with a different woman on his arm.

Of course, later on in August, she'd been surprised by Carrie and Trent's sudden and unexpected marriage. Jacinda knew Carrie had taken a dim view of Trent's antics. Even so, she hadn't felt close enough to the other woman to ask her about swiftly tying the knot.

"Do you think you'll be able to attend on New Year's Eve, Gage?" Carrie asked.

"Planning to," Gage responded with a smile.

"And who knows?" Reed put in with a sly look. "Maybe Gage will surprise us and bring a date."

Gage quirked an eyebrow at Reed, and Jacinda caught Amanda smiling at her.

Jacinda looked down into the glass she was holding.

Did Gage's neighbors suspect something was going on between her and her tight-lipped billionaire employer? If so, wouldn't they be surprised to discover her true identity!

"It's so nice to have some good news in this building, after Marie Endicott's tragic death last summer, poor girl," Elizabeth commented.

Jacinda suddenly tensed.

"The police think it was foul play," Reed said. "But they're still looking for the missing videotape of the roof from the night in question."

"Of course, they think it's foul play!" Amanda put in. "They know someone has tried to blackmail us, and, of course, Julia. Something fishy is going on."

Jacinda supposed the building residents around her were comfortable discussing the blackmail schemes amongst themselves because they'd all been targets.

"The police investigation has been frustratingly slow," Carrie noted.

Silently, Jacinda echoed those sentiments. She'd had her own issues with the police.

"Detective McGray is overworked and underpaid," Elizabeth said, "and he's the one looking into both the blackmail and Marie's death."

Gage nodded. "They'll get to the bottom of it soon."

Over Gage's shoulder, Jacinda noticed Vivian Vannick-Smythe slip away from the party and head toward the front door.

She'd hardly had a chance to say anything to the older woman all evening, but she supposed it was just as well. What would they have to talk about anyway? She'd always gotten the uncomfortable sense Vivian could see through her facade.

"Unfortunately, I need to leave," Amanda said, checking her watch. "I'm working with a new client tomorrow who's throwing a big bash at the 21 Club next week." She looked at Jacinda and winked. "Great party. If you're ever looking for a new line of work, let me know."

"I'll do that," Jacinda heard herself respond. She felt like such a phony.

Soon thereafter, the other guests began to take their leave, and Jacinda went back to the kitchen area to supervise the caterers and bartenders as they cleaned up.

At some point, she looked up to see Gage chatting at the front door with a couple of the lingering guests— Carrie and Trent Tanford. And a little while later, she noticed Gage assisting in the winding-down effort by helping the musicians put the furniture back to rights after they had broken down their equipment.

Not for the first time, she reflected that Gage was surprisingly down-to-earth for a billionaire to-the-manor-born.

And again the thought made her smile.

Half an hour later, however, she found herself feeling less relaxed.

The last of the hired staff for the evening had just departed, and she was alone with Gage.

Christmas music played from the speakers in the apartment, and she could see Gage in the kitchen, fiddling with a bottle of wine and a corkscrew at the kitchen counter.

He looked up, and she swallowed against a suddenly dry throat.

"Well, I'm going to head to bed," she said.

Bed. Wrong word. Especially since she'd been having shocking and recurring thoughts of Gage and a bed for too long.

Gage's lips twisted into a smile. "Stay and have a celebratory drink with me for a party well-done."

"You don't need to thank me," she said, wetting her lips. "It's my job."

"Okay," he responded agreeably, "so let's say instead we're having one last one for the road."

"We're both sleeping here," she pointed out. Together but in separate beds.

"So we are," he replied with another easy smile. "But it's a big penthouse, and it can be a long walk back to the bedroom."

She was defenseless against this new charming and flirtatious Gage.

"Okay," she heard herself say.

Gage picked up the uncorked wine bottle in one hand and two glasses by the stems in the other. "Come sit on the couch."

The couch? She was in trouble.

"I saved the best for last," Gage said as he came around the kitchen counter.

"What?" she squeaked.

He looked at her innocently. "My best wine label."

"Oh, right."

How silly of her to think he'd meant anything else…

Outside, the lights of Manhattan twinkled back at them, visible through the draped French windows of Gage's living room.

Inside was another matter, Jacinda thought. As the sound of Johnny Mathis filtered through the apartment, she was much too tense to play in a winter wonderland. She was too aware of Gage's long, lean body settling down next to her on the couch, after he'd handed her a wineglass.

"Good party," Gage said. "Congratulations."

She took a sip of her wine to ease her nerves. "It's easy to throw a good party when you have an almost limitless budget."

His eyes crinkled in amusement, his dimple showing. "I wouldn't say limitless," he demurred. "And the party was some work. Don't sell yourself short. I just hope you enjoyed yourself a little, too."

"I did."

He tilted his head. "Yes, I saw you speaking with Steve Floyd."

A smile rose to her lips. She hadn't had a date since…well, since before Marie's death. It had been nice to forget her troubles for a moment and allow an attractive man to flirt with her. Plus, ever since starting her masquerade as a maid, she'd had a soft spot for anyone who treated the hired help well.

"Steve's wonderful," she said. "He's got the most outrageous only-in-New-York stories."

"Don't like him too much," Gage replied. "Steve's a notorious love 'em-and-leave 'em type."

"And you're not?"

The words were out of her mouth before she could stop them.

He looked at her meaningfully. "Sweetheart, I haven't had a date since before picnic blankets dotted Central Park last summer. In case you haven't noticed, I've been traveling a lot in the past few months. Work's been…well, work."

The word *sweetheart* shimmied down her spine in a bold caress, and then hot pricks of awareness zipped through her.

Was he flirting with her?

As if in answer to her question, Gage cocked his head. "You know you intrigue me, Jane."

"Do I?"

Gage nodded thoughtfully. "You're obviously skilled and knowledgeable, and you have a keen mind. Why be a housekeeper?"

Before she could answer, however, he looked her over. "How old are you?"

"Twenty-nine."

And he was thirty-five, as she'd discovered while compiling her dossier on him.

"You've got your whole life ahead of you," he said.

Yes, she thought. Unlike Marie, who'd had her life snuffed out.

She felt her heart squeeze, and sudden emotion clogged her throat at the thought of her sister.

It was the holidays, and she was hundreds of miles away from her remaining family, on a mission that had so far gotten her nowhere.

She cleared her throat.

"Maybe I'm a bit of a free spirit," she said with forced flippancy. "I get to live in an ever-changing series of luxurious homes that are well beyond what I could afford on my own."

Her response sounded convincing to her. She hoped he thought it was, too.

Before he could respond, though, she turned the conversation in a safer direction.

"What about you?" she asked. "You're working hard. You admitted you haven't had a date since before summer."

He took a sip of his wine. "Ah, but that's the result of having had a taste of betrayal that's not easily forgotten."

She wondered whether he was referring to his ex-wife. If he'd had a taste of female treachery, what would he think of her masquerade?

He added, "So, you could say my situation is more

a deliberately chosen path rather than an aimless wandering."

"Ah."

He bent forward and set his wineglass down on a nearby surface.

Then he turned and took hers from her suddenly nerveless fingers and set it down beside its companion.

When he turned back to her, she sucked in a breath at the look in his eyes.

Her heart beat faster as he leaned forward and cupped her face in his hands.

"W-what are you doing?" she asked.

"Making another deliberate choice," he murmured against her mouth. "It looks like my path's led to your door. Consider this the kiss hello."

Her eyes closed as his mouth settled over hers. His lips stroked in a slow, sensual greeting.

The kiss sent tingles of awareness shooting through her.

His fingers combed through her hair, cupping her head and bringing her closer.

Her mouth opened to him, letting him take the kiss deeper and stoke the attraction between them. He tasted of wine, and she picked up a scent that was warm and all male.

Jacinda thought hazily that she hadn't felt this good in a long time. She leaned into Gage and sighed, feeling her nipples harden.

Eventually, Gage slowed the kiss down, lightening his touch, and when they broke apart, Jacinda became aware of the heavy, rhythmic beat of her heart.

"Let's just grab at some happiness," Gage murmured against her mouth, his eyes heavy-lidded.

Why not?

They were the first words to spring into her head.

She was having a hard time remembering why she should resist her attraction to him. She was almost certain now that Gage wasn't the perpetrator of her sister's murder or of the blackmail at 721 Park Avenue.

The truth was they were two souls alone and lonely at the holidays.

And she'd fought so hard against her attraction to Gage for the past several months. Why deny herself some comfort now?

She gave the barest nod of her head, and it was all the encouragement he needed.

And then they were kissing again, with renewed urgency this time.

Her arms moved around his neck, and he pulled her forward across his lap.

His tongue entered her mouth, encouraging her to mate with him in an erotic dance that was a precursor of another.

She couldn't get close enough to him. She felt his erection against her and shifted even closer.

Being in his arms was a surprising oasis of light and calm in a world that had been topsy-turvy for the past six months.

She felt herself floating up, carried on the wings of pleasurable sensation, as she shed all the troubles that had been shackling her, weighing her down, for the past half year.

He slowed enough to toy with her mouth.

"Gage," she breathed.

His eyes were hooded, dark with desire.

"Yes," he said huskily. "Sweetheart, let me pleasure you. I've been wanting to for so long."

His words thrilled her. "Yes, Gage."

He stood and swung her up into his arms.

"What are you doing?" she asked, her voice breathy.

"Taking you to bed," he responded in a tone rough with desire. "My bed."

Yes.

In the background, Dean Martin crooned "Baby, It's Cold Outside."

Yes, it was a cold world out there, but here, inside, she was sheltered in Gage's arms.

He carried her up the stairs to the penthouse's upper level, and all the while she reveled in the strong, steady beat of his heart against her.

When he reached the upper floor, he strode along the corridor and kicked open the door to the master bedroom, and then deposited her next to the bed.

Jacinda had been inside Gage's bedroom dozens of times, and now the impressions came back to her without effort. Recessed lighting, polished wood floors, and modern furniture. A large bed resting on a mahogany platform. Five-hundred-count luxury French linens.

Gage stepped behind her, and Jacinda felt little shivers of awareness dance along her skin.

Gently, he moved her curtain of hair aside so that it rested over one shoulder, the back of his hand caressing the side of her neck as he did so.

And then his hands closed over her bare shoulders, and he trailed moist kisses from the base of her neck to the hollow behind her ear.

She moaned, and her head fell back, giving him better access.

When he nipped her earlobe, and then blew softly in her ear, hot sensations shot through her.

She leaned back against him.

"Easy," he breathed.

She felt him find the zipper that started at the back of her neck, and then listened to it rasp downward as cool air hit her back.

She trembled.

"Cold?" he murmured.

She wanted to tell him it was what *he* was doing that was giving her goose bumps.

Before she could react, however, the gas fireplace along the wall behind her roared to life, and she realized he must have hit a switch somewhere.

He pushed the dress off her shoulders and it pooled at her feet, around her black pumps.

She felt vulnerable…and excited.

His hands trailed over the indentation of her waist, smoothed over the curves of her thighs and then caressed her stocking-clad legs.

Eventually, they wandered back up to cup her breasts, and she felt his erection press against her again.

He trailed the tips of both index fingers along the top edges of her black demi-bra cups, and then underneath, along the underwire.

She didn't have the most voluptuous of figures, but he made her feel wild and wanton.

"Ah, sweetheart," he said. "You tempt me."

And he made her ache.

When he finally cupped both breasts, she sighed and then savored the feeling of him stroking and kneading them.

As if sensing her complete capitulation was near, he nipped her earlobe, and then ran the tip of his tongue along the delicate shell of her ear, rocking against her from behind.

His hands stroked over her body, igniting a fire as they went.

She groaned and reached up behind her to cup the back of his head and draw him closer.

He nuzzled her neck. "So good."

"Mmm…"

Her legs felt rubbery, as if they'd give way at any moment.

His hands smoothed down over her hips, taking her underwear with them. And then one hand splayed across her abdomen while the other cupped her intimately.

She moaned and shifted, affording him better access as her eyelids lowered.

His fingers played in her moist heat, making her dizzy with passion.

"Gage, I don't know how much more I can take."

"We're just getting started."

"That's what I'm afraid of." Lava flowed through her veins.

He gave a low chuckle. "Step out of those naughty give-it-to-me heels."

"Is that a demand?" she asked breathlessly.

"Take it however you want it, sweetheart, but know the chase is over."

She did as he asked, and then pulled off her thigh-high stockings, as well.

He reached to the middle of her back and unclasped her bra. As she lowered her arms, the garment slithered to the floor, and he turned her around.

She watched as his heated look traveled down her body and then back up to meet her eyes.

"You're beautiful…and sexy as hell."

He made her feel beautiful. Instead of replying, however, she bunched her fist in his white shirt front and pulled him toward her.

She kissed him with all the passion he'd stoked in her.

At first, she tasted surprise in his kiss, but it was quickly replaced by an intense ardor.

When they finally broke apart, they were both breathing deeply.

She kicked off her shoes, and everything—shoes, dress and underwear—went sliding across the polished wood floor.

He picked her up then and laid her on the bed, and she savored the feeling of being cradled in his arms again.

When he straightened, standing at the foot of the bed, he made rapid work of his own clothes, his eyes glittering down at her, full of passion and fire.

His movements were clipped, rough, as he unbuttoned his shirt and yanked it off. His undershirt came up over his head, and he tossed it aside.

She soaked in the sight of him shirtless, admiring the defined muscles in his arms and chest.

He undid his watch and tossed it on the bed. Then his hands went to his belt, and once he'd removed it, he kicked off his shoes and socks and lowered his black trousers.

Her breath hissed in as she took in the sight of him in black banded briefs.

But suddenly he looked beyond her, toward the other side of the bed, and frowned. "Damn it, I don't remember where I put protection."

"Second drawer, night table on the right," she replied.

She knew where she'd last seen some condoms. She was familiar with everything about his apartment.

Gage studied her, and then his face broke into a grin, his dimple showing through. "I knew there were benefits to sleeping with my housekeeper."

She arched a brow. "Done it before?"

He grinned again. "Sweetheart, you're my first."

He looked boyish and carefree, so different from his usual, guarded self that her heart flipped over.

She watched as he reached over and pulled open the nightstand drawer, searched inside for a moment with his hand and then pulled out a foil packet.

When he turned back to her, he tore open the packet and she sat up on the bed and reached for him.

Without waiting for an invitation, she pulled down his briefs and let his erection spring free.

She watched as the muscles of his stomach tensed, and then she reached out and began to stroke him.

The breath hissed out of him, but when she looked up to meet his gaze, his hooded eyes were full of lambent fire.

"Sweetheart, ah…"

Moments ticked by, and his breathing grew more harsh, fevering her own arousal.

Finally, he grasped her wrist and stilled her.

He quickly donned the protection and tossed the foil wrapper aside.

As she leaned back, he stretched out on the bed beside her.

Her hands played over the muscles of his shoulders and back while he caressed and kissed her.

When she was desperate for him to take her, however, he surprised her by moving her to her side and shifting behind her, spooning her.

Hooking her upper leg over his, he tested and found her moist heat. As she gasped, he nipped her neck and then slowly slid into her welcoming warmth.

"Gage…" Her voice trailed off as liquid fire suffused her. This position was new to her.

His hand stole around to touch her from the front, making her experience every exquisite sensation in a burst of color.

He slid in and out of her, and they both moaned with every brief joining.

Jacinda had never gotten aroused so quickly, had never experienced such a rapid and heady spring to complete abandon.

"Give yourself to me," Gage murmured.

His rough words were her undoing, and she flowered for him, moving against him, in a sudden burst of energy.

Her long, drawn-out moan made his muscles tense.

He gripped her hip and his fingers flexed as he drove into her with a harsh groan.

Moments later, they both sagged against the mattress.

It was then that the notes of "Have Yourself a Merry Little Christmas" reached her, and tears sprang to her eyes.

Four

He woke up feeling sated.

No, even better, Gage corrected himself as he opened his eyes. He felt content.

And it was all due to Jane.

He glanced over at the other side of the bed—which was empty.

Jane had already gotten up, which was quite a feat since he was an early riser himself.

Raising his head, he noted the clock on the bedside table revealed it was half past six. And since he could smell coffee brewing, Jane must already be getting breakfast ready.

Gage settled back against his pillow and stretched. One thing was certain in the clear light of day. He should have given in to the attraction between him and Jane a lot sooner.

He'd never cared what other people would think of him sleeping with his housekeeper. He was rich enough not to give a damn, and long past the point of needing social approval.

And Jane was genuine—the real deal. Unlike so many women he knew. Unlike his ex-wife, for example.

Now, he didn't know why he'd fought against the attraction to Jane for so long.

Turning his thoughts in an even more pleasant direction, he contemplated whisking Jane off to his hideaway in Bermuda for the forthcoming weekend. They could both get a respite from Manhattan—which overflowed with tourists during the holiday season—and escape to a balmy climate.

He wondered what Jane would say to the plan, and then grinned. At least he wouldn't have to worry about her work schedule. He'd be more than happy to give her a few days off to get away from it all with him.

With that thought, he rose and threw on some sweatpants.

When he padded downstairs, he discovered Jane in the kitchen, her back to him and talking in a low voice into her cell phone.

It was apparent she hadn't heard him come down.

His gaze swept over her, and he felt the kick of arousal.

She must have found some clothes in her room because she was dressed in a knee-length satin robe. The robe, however, did little to hide her assets. Instead, it showcased an hourglass figure and outlined a rounded bottom.

Her hair tumbled over her shoulders, and slim, shapely legs seemed to go on forever.

Desire slammed into him.

He wanted to take her again right here, right now.

Then a couple of her words reached him, and abruptly he frowned.

He was standing a few feet away, and he realized he didn't recognize the voice she was using.

Her accent was…British.

He stepped closer.

"Do the police know anything else about Marie's death?"

Gage stilled.

"It's so frustrating. I know our sister didn't take her own life."

Gage's eyes narrowed. What the hell did Jane mean by *sister?*

She was obviously talking about Marie Endicott— the broker whom he'd hired and whose death the police had ruled suspicious.

But if Jane was Marie's sister, why hadn't she said anything?

His mind zipped through the possibilities, and he didn't like any of them.

And as his suspicion grew, so did a simmering anger.

It was looking like he'd been taken for a ride. By a woman. Again.

He must have made a sound, because suddenly Jane whirled around, her eyes wide.

Shock flitted across her features, but was quickly replaced by alarm.

Gage would have thought the reaction was comical, if he hadn't been at the receiving end of it.

"Andrew, I must go." She spoke into the receiver, but her eyes were fixed on him.

As soon as Jane ended her call, he didn't wait for an invitation.

"Who the hell are you?" he demanded.

Her lips parted. "I—"

He could practically see the wheels turning in her head, as if she was trying to guess how much he'd heard and come up with something to say.

The realization only made him more furious.

"Wait, I know," he said sarcastically, answering his own question. "You're Marie Endicott's sister."

He watched as Jane went pale. Except, he realized, he wasn't even sure anymore that her name was Jane.

She seemed to come to some kind of resolution, and her chin lifted. "My name is Jacinda Endicott."

"Nice British accent," he commented. "Now, mind telling me what the hell you're doing playing maid?"

She squared her shoulders. "I can explain, if only you'll let me."

Under other circumstances, he might have admired her bravado. But this situation hit too close to home. He'd let her get under his skin, damn it.

He folded his arms. "This ought to be good."

She took a deep breath. "I came here because I knew from the beginning my sister couldn't have killed herself. But I was desperate because the police had ruled it a suicide."

She spoke quickly, as if she believed that at any moment he'd give her the boot from the apartment. In that, he acknowledged, she wasn't too far off.

"What does this have to do with me?" he demanded.

"I decided to take matters into my own hands—"

"By posing as a maid in the building so you could do some snooping?" he finished for her.

She hesitated, then nodded. "Yes."

She looked vulnerable and sexy as hell. Even now, he couldn't help his instinctual reaction to her effortless sexuality.

"Why me?" he demanded. "Out of all the residents in this building?"

"I discovered you and Marie had known each other," she admitted in a low voice.

He nodded curtly. "Right. She was my real estate agent. I was impressed by her energy and hired her despite the fact that she was young and relatively inexperienced."

He watched as Jacinda bit her lip.

"I thought you and Marie were...involved."

Realization dawned, and with it, his anger kicked up a notch. "Are you telling me you suspected I had something to do with your sister's death?"

When she nodded, he stared at her disbelievingly.

He'd trusted her, damn it.

"You slept with me and all the while you thought I had something to do with your sister's death?" he asked incredulously.

"I'd ruled you out by that point," she said, her voice suddenly heated.

"Oh, yeah? How? By finding the killer?"

"Aside from being a client, I couldn't find any evidence linking you to Marie!"

"Great, just great. I've been legit with you from the beginning and, all the while, you've been playing detective."

She hugged herself. "The longer I looked without turning up anything, the less likely it was you were the…one responsible."

His lip curled. Apparently she couldn't bring herself to say the word *murderer.*

"I've searched Marie's apartment," she went on, "and so did the police, to no avail. I've also been to my sister's old office, where her coworker took over the lease and is still running a real estate business. Nothing."

He'd heard murmurings through the building grapevine that Marie's old apartment on the sixth floor hadn't been sold yet. Now he knew why. Jacinda was still hoping for clues.

"So that's what you were doing when you forgot to dust the bookcases or scrub the sink around here," he accused, piecing it together. "And here I was wondering why you were a maid instead of an aspiring starlet, like everyone else in New York. I didn't know you were already putting your acting skills to good use!"

She started, a guilty look on her face, but then continued determinedly, "Yesterday I got a call from my brother in London, who's in touch with the police. He told me about the attempted blackmails in the building, and how the police's new theory is that an insider was behind both the blackmail and Marie's murder."

He arched a brow.

She dropped her arms. "I knew you couldn't be a blackmailer. You don't need the money. It didn't make any sense!"

"And do you also know I was a victim of one of the blackmail plots?" he asked icily.

She shook her head, looking at him helplessly.

"Oh, yes, indeed," he said, his voice dripping sarcasm. "Reed Wellington was blackmailed, and when he refused to pay, it appears someone went to the Securities and Exchange Commission with the false story that he and I had benefited from an insider stock tip."

They stared at each other.

His jaw hardened. "I should fire you on the spot."

He could fire her, but, he acknowledged, he couldn't as easily eradicate her from his life. Her scent was on his skin. Her stamp was on his apartment. She'd infiltrated the inner sanctum of his life.

"How did you get Theresa to recommend you?" he demanded, having a perverse urge to know all the details, now that her secret was out.

She opened her mouth, and then hesitated.

"Don't even think about not telling me the whole deal," he ordered.

She stopped, blinked, her brow furrowing. "I got a friend to provide a false reference, and I let Theresa think my mother had attended her high school alma mater on Long Island."

"Clever." He didn't mean it as a compliment, and

she seemed to know better than to acknowledge it as such.

"I was going to tell you…"

"Sure," he snarled. "And should I assume last night was about softening me up for your pitch?"

He had the satisfaction of seeing her turn pale again.

"Last night, when Marie's death came up, you said nothing," he said, his voice clipped.

"I wasn't going to tell you who I really was in front of half the residents of the building!"

"And all that stuff about being a free spirit," he went on, his lip curling. "It was all a pack of lies."

Alarm and then guilt crossed her face.

"It's actually a bit of a family trait," she said, barely above a whisper.

"The free-spiritedness or the lying?"

She blanched, and his jaw tightened.

"Why the hell would you make the leap from Marie being my real estate broker to thinking I had something to do with her death?"

He couldn't get himself to say *murderer,* either.

She looked close to tears. "Marie was having an affair. She was so closemouthed, I only discovered it after her death, from one of her coworkers. Marie had described the man as a very rich and powerful loner. Someone who was tall and dark, and had a noticeable dimple."

"And from that you concluded the man was *me?*" he said incredulously.

"I thought it was the perfect cover. The phone calls ostensibly about finding new real estate for you when in reality—"

"We were conducting a clandestine affair?" he said in disbelief. "Did it ever occur to you that where there's smoke, there may not be fire?"

"I know it sounds batty now—"

"It's off the wall!"

"—but I was overcome with grief at losing my sister. I knew she didn't kill herself."

"And that's your explanation for lying and deceiving me?" he demanded. "For coming here under false pretenses?"

"I need your help," she pleaded.

He admired her audacity, while her nerve infuriated him.

He spread his hands. "Sorry, can't help," he bit out. "Until recently, I was a suspect, remember?"

"I don't know where else to turn," she said, her voice tinged with desperation. "The police now think Marie's death is suspicious—"

"So I've heard."

"—but they don't have any leads."

"Yeah," he taunted, "and if you'd come clean about who you were, maybe we'd have linked Marie's death to the blackmail schemes earlier."

"Would you have listened to me?" she flung back at him, and then shook her head, as if answering her own question. "No, I don't think so. Even the police were maintaining Marie's death was a suicide."

Would he have listened to her? The truth was, he let himself acknowledge, he'd have been leery of another blond bombshell with an agenda.

He contemplated her. She was supplicating, on the point of begging him, really.

She was also the woman who'd made sweet, passionate love with him mere hours ago. The woman he'd let his guard down with.

And despite his best intentions, he wasn't unmoved by her plea. He still wanted her.

He cursed under his breath.

Then he realized that while he might still want her, she *needed* him. And with that, an idea started to form.

He wiped his face clean of emotion—the way he often did with an adversary across the bargaining table.

"You need my help," he said calmly.

She nodded, her expression wary.

"I could lean on the police, use my contacts—"

She nodded again. "Yes, exactly."

"For a price."

Her eyes widened.

"I don't have anything to give," she said, startled. "If it's money—"

"No."

She shook her head. "I make good money as an ad executive, but nothing on the order to tempt a billionaire." She paused. "What do you want, then?"

"You," he said flatly. "I want you."

She sucked in a breath. "What?"

"You heard me," he said, his voice hard. "I want you in my bed."

She looked astounded. "You want to buy me…like an investment property or an art object?"

"I prefer the term *mistress*," he said dryly.

Her mouth opened and shut.

"Are you married? Engaged? Steady boyfriend?" he asked brusquely.

She shook her head.

Some of his tension ebbed. "Well then, there should be no problem."

"You can't be serious!"

"You want my cooperation, that's my price. Of course, I'll hire a cleaning service to take over maintenance of the apartment."

Their eyes locked, and several taut moments passed.

Finally, she said in a low voice, "I'm willing to do whatever it takes."

His gaze swept over her. "Oh, sweetheart, you have what it takes."

And then he decided to give her a taste of what to expect.

He reached out and pulled her into his embrace.

He took in her wide, startled eyes and parted lips before his mouth crushed hers.

The kiss was hard and unyielding. A stamp of possession neither of them could mistake.

Her soft curves pressed against him, making him want, making him burn.

His tongue swept into her mouth, and fireworks erupted, just as they had the night before.

But after a moment, he let her break free.

She stepped back, and covered her mouth with her hand.

They stared at each other and moments later, she lowered her hand.

"Make no mistake," she said. "You'll get my body, but that's all you'll get."

She brushed past him, and he turned and watched as she fled toward the back of the penthouse.

Toward the maid's quarters, where she no longer belonged.

Crossing a billionaire had been even more ghastly than she'd expected, Jacinda thought, still in the process of straightening up the kitchen counter.

It was past ten in the evening, and she was restless. Gage had left a note this morning saying not to bother with dinner for him because he'd be meeting a business associate.

She found it lonely, rattling around by herself in an apartment that was bigger than many homes.

Outside, the city lights twinkled, and inside, the Christmas decorations cast a warm glow.

Most visitors to New York would be enjoying themselves right now. It was the season when thousands of tourists flocked to the city for holiday shopping and shows, filling restaurants and hotels, and spilling into the streets and onto double-decker tour buses.

But Jacinda knew her feelings had nothing to do with the season, and everything to do with a certain billionaire.

She squeezed her eyes shut for a moment as she remembered her confrontation with Gage two days ago.

She'd made a mess of things. She'd gone about it all wrong from the beginning.

She should have confessed to Gage who she was before he'd found out himself in the worst possible way.

She winced as she thought back to how angry Gage had been.

Then again, she tried telling herself, even if she had come clean, Gage would have been just as furious at being duped. The only thing she could have hoped for was that when she begged for his help, he would have been swayed a little by the fact she'd come forward by choice.

She placed a couple of pots back in the cupboard.

As it was, she'd bargained with the devil.

I prefer the term mistress.

His words came back to her, reverberating in her mind, as they had for the last forty-eight hours.

She'd sold herself in exchange for his help.

"Billionaire's mistress." She tried out the title on her tongue.

Never, never, never in her wildest dreams would she have thought she'd acquire that title. But then again, six months ago, she hadn't known any billionaires.

If only her friends and colleagues could see her now.

Of course, her family would be aghast. One daughter dead, and now the other a kept woman.

Her family would think she was out of her league with Gage Lattimer—which was, of course, true.

Gage.

She couldn't believe his cold-bloodedness.

He'd propositioned her with cool calculation.

She could well understand now how he'd made hundreds of millions betting on and trading in start-up companies. He had a quick, analytical mind, true, but he was also one cool customer.

While she'd been doing her best not to fall for him these past months, he'd apparently been unmoved. As soon as her real identity had come out, he'd switched to propositioning her, without missing a beat.

She was mortified…and angry.

Oh, she knew she wasn't an innocent party herself, but even though her head was telling her to be rational, her heart couldn't help feeling hurt.

Had their night of passion meant nothing more to him than a roll between the sheets with the hired help? Apparently so, since he'd handed her a take-it-or-leave-it offer.

And she'd had to take it. She didn't have much confidence in the police cracking this case—at least not without help and outside pressure—and she was willing to do whatever it took to see that Marie got justice.

She *needed* Gage's money, power and influence.

But more than that, the most damning thing was she didn't mind as much as she should going back to Gage's bed.

Their night together had been a revelation. She'd never felt such a swift, overpowering attraction to a man before. A man who had proved to be an expert, imaginative lover.

She heated up as images from their night of passion in Gage's bed flashed through her mind. After their initial coming together, they'd woken up and had sex once more. Gage had caused responses from her body that she didn't know it was capable of.

She was glad now, however, that she'd vowed to close her heart to him. He might get her body, but he wouldn't get anything else.

Fortunately, he hadn't pressed the matter since their confrontation. She'd gone back to the maid's room and stayed there.

It was as if he sensed they both needed a cooling off period—like two boxers going back to their corners.

Or more aptly, like two lovers recovering from a spat.

As if conjured by her thoughts, she heard the front door click and turned to see Gage step inside the apartment.

He stilled when he spotted her, and then proceeded to shed his coat.

"We're going to Bermuda," he announced without preamble.

Her lips parted. She'd expected more of the cool distance of the past forty-eight hours. Not this.

He deposited his coat and briefcase on a nearby chair.

"First thing in the morning," he elaborated as he moved toward her. "I have a house there."

Of course, she knew that. She knew all about his various and far-flung real estate holdings.

"Ever been?"

She shook her head.

His lips twisted in the semblance of a smile. "Well, don't worry. You'll feel right at home. They drive on the right side of the road, like in London."

Of course, she knew. Bermuda was a British territory in the Atlantic.

He stopped on the other side of the kitchen counter. "Where's your luggage?"

She found her voice. "It's at the studio apartment I sublet on York Avenue."

He nodded curtly, as if absorbing an additional detail about her and her elaborately planned masquerade of the last few months.

"You can use one of my suitcases," he said.

"I don't have much here appropriate for Bermuda's warm weather."

His lips twisted again. "Don't worry. You can buy stuff when we get there and charge it to me."

She felt herself flush at the reminder of the arrangement she'd agreed to. "Why are we going?"

He looked at her penetratingly. "Because I've been working too hard, and I need some R & R."

She wondered what else he needed besides rest and relaxation, and she could tell from the look on his face he knew where her thoughts were heading.

She schooled her features, refusing to give him the satisfaction of knowing he'd rattled her. "And how are we getting there?"

"My jet. From La Guardia. You could say I'm driving."

Of course. She knew he had a pilot's license.

"I see."

"Don't worry," he added, his voice mocking. "There's also a copilot and a skeleton crew."

She finally felt a rise of anger. "That's not what I'm concerned about. I thought you were going to help me solve my sister's murder."

"And I thought *you* agreed to becoming my mistress."

"Yes, but not to jetting off to Bermuda," she replied.

"Worried about the Bermuda Triangle? Don't fret, sweetheart. I've flown through it a couple dozen times. You're in good hands."

"Oh, of course," she retorted. "I mistakenly assumed this was a plot to get rid of me."

He flashed her a mirthless smile.

"What I meant is," she went on coolly, "how are we going to solve anything if we're in Bermuda?"

"I've already spoken to the police. Detective McGray."

She stared at him in surprise. "What? When?"

"From work." He looked at her mockingly. "You didn't expect I'd have you sitting nearby, listening in on every word, did you?"

Damn him. "What did you tell him?"

"Nothing about your little masquerade." He added dryly, "I doubt McGray and the NYPD would appreciate knowing you've been encroaching on their territory by playing detective."

She supposed she should be thankful to him for not betraying her. But the words stuck in her throat.

"I informed Detective McGray that I've taken a very personal interest in the Marie Endicott case," he elaborated, seeming to have some mercy on her, "and I want it solved. I don't care how many detectives they need to throw at it. I also let it slip I'm good buddies with the mayor, the police commissioner and everyone in between."

Her shoulders lowered as some of her tension ebbed.

Gage shrugged. "I contribute generously to political and charitable causes in the city."

"Thank you for your help," she said huskily.

He nodded curtly, and then moved by her toward the stairs.

"Sweet dreams, Jacinda," he said. "I'm looking forward to our trip."

As Jacinda watched him go, she thought he might as well have said, *I'm looking forward to having you uphold your end of the bargain.*

Any other woman would have been thrilled at the prospect of jetting off to an island paradise with a good-looking, virile billionaire.

Not her, she told herself. Not under these circumstances.

Life had a quirky sense of humor, she acknowledged, even as, at the same time, she felt an odd flutter at the thought of a romantic idyll with Gage.

Five

He was a bastard.

And the one thing about piloting your own private jet for a couple of hours, Gage thought, was that it gave you plenty of time to dwell on just what a bastard you were.

He stared out the cockpit at the endless sky before him, checking monitors and controls regularly as he did so. His copilot—one of the private contractors who often worked for him—had stepped back into the cabin for a brief break.

But Gage knew his fiftyish copilot would be back soon. In a short while, they'd begin their descent to Bermuda.

In the meantime, he could sit back and try to enjoy flying. Usually he loved the sense of freedom that came with it. He thrived on it, in fact. It was a brief respite from feeling tethered to his numerous responsibilities.

But, on this trip, there was one responsibility he *hadn't* left behind.

She was, in fact, sitting in the cabin behind him, no doubt contemplating the bargain she'd struck.

Jacinda.

He was still getting used to her name on his tongue—after she'd sidelined him with her bombshell revelations.

Jacinda. Her real name.

It suited her better than Jane. *Jacinda* came from the Greek for *hyacinth,* he knew, for once grateful for having been forced to study the classics at prep school.

It seemed appropriate she was named after the fragrant flower. He intended to savor her scent—and everything else—during this trip. He wanted to make her bloom for him.

These past couple of days, he'd also discovered he liked her natural British accent a lot more than her contrived American one, and grudgingly admitted she must have a good ear for accents to be such a good mimic.

In fact, he found her British voice sexy and distracting.

He ought to be mad as hell at her deception. He was, but the initial searing anger had passed. Unlike his ex-wife, at least Jacinda had been motivated in her deception by overwhelming grief.

He supposed, if he'd had a sister, he'd have been just as intent on discovering the truth behind her tragic death.

Even the police now believed Marie's death to be suspicious. And with good reason, Gage thought, his expression darkening as he recalled the blackmail plots that had come to light.

He thought back to his call to Detective McGray, a midlife veteran of the NYPD.

Gage was familiar with the career detective's type. As soon as he'd made it clear how connected he was, he knew he'd gotten McGray's attention. In no uncertain terms, he'd delivered the message that he expected the guy to stop hitting the snooze button on this case.

And by the middle of the call, Gage could have sworn he heard the detective's feet hitting the floor from their position on some battered metal desk.

He told himself all of it had been done in return for Jacinda becoming his mistress.

He'd been so furious with her when she'd poured forth the truth. Furious at her for her deception. Furious at himself for wanting her all the same.

So he'd decided punishment was in order, though it was a toss up as to whom he was punishing by demanding she become his mistress.

She hadn't been too happy about his proposition. And for his part, he'd have to continue fighting getting overpowered by a bad case of the hots.

He'd never felt such a swift, overpowering lust for any other woman. It kicked in at the mere sight of her, and their round in bed a couple of nights ago had served to sharpen his desire rather than quench it.

As his copilot stepped back into the cockpit and Gage prepared the jet for the descent to Bermuda's L.F.

Wade International Airport, he wondered how far he was willing to take his arrangement with Jacinda.

He wasn't any closer to an answer hours later, after they'd landed and arrived at his villa along Bermuda's southwest coast.

He did, however, instruct the staff to place Jacinda's suitcase in the master suite. He watched as after a brief hesitation, Jacinda walked toward their shared bedroom to unpack.

Afterward, the two of them had lunch, and then he had to take some business-related calls.

At some point, he observed through a window that Jacinda was exploring the house and grounds.

When the sun was ready to set, however, he found her curled up with a book in the sitting area of the master suite.

She was dressed in a knee-length sleeveless cotton sundress with a flower print and halter-top. He'd called ahead and made sure his staff had made some rudimentary purchases for her so she'd have something appropriate to wear when she first arrived.

He'd changed and showered also since their flight, and had donned some sand-colored chinos, an open-collar blue shirt and a pair of nautical-style brown moccasins.

"Come sit out here and watch the sunset with me," he said, sliding back the doors leading from the master suite to an outdoor terrace. "We'll sip some wine before dinner."

He watched her hesitate before nodding and coming toward him.

"Planning to ply me with alcohol before you have

your way with me?" she asked tartly as she stepped onto the terrace along with him.

He saw beyond the false bravado. She was nervous.

He set down an ice bucket with a bottle of white wine and two glasses that he'd had a member of the staff deliver to the master suite earlier.

"Now is that any way to show your gratitude?" he asked mildly, his tone faintly mocking.

He was mocking not only her, but their situation.

He added, "I see you found some of the clothes I instructed the staff to purchase."

"Yes, it was…thoughtful of you."

"I admit to being surprised you chose the halter-top."

She was clearly braless underneath, and the airy cotton fabric skimmed her trim figure.

He felt a kick-start and then a tightening in his gut.

"I decided to dress the part."

Neither of them needed to give voice to what part she was referring to. Mistress.

His lips quirked up. "You're doing a good job."

She met his gaze. "Or at least, what I think is the part. I have no idea how to act like a mistress."

A half smile crossed his lips as he poured the wine into two glasses.

"Likewise," he said, handing her a glass. "You're my first."

She looked surprised as she took the glass from him. Their hands brushed, causing her to bobble the glass for a second.

"Ex-wife, yes. Mistress, no," he elaborated.

"How is that possible?"

"Simple," he said. "I date discriminately, but I haven't had any interest in having a particular woman at my…disposal."

Until now. For a price.

He watched as she flushed at the reference to her new status as a kept woman—her bills paid, her needs taken care of.

"How did you know my dress size?"

"I checked the clothes in your room before we left New York."

She gaped at him.

"Did you think you were the only one capable of rifling through someone's personal possessions?" he asked.

She flushed again.

The truth was he'd done some extensive digging of his own.

"I also know you're an ad executive with Winter & Baker back in London," he said.

"Currently on leave."

"Right," he responded, inclining his head. "Impressive position, though."

"I'm good at what I do."

He raised his glass to her in silent salute. "I've always admired people who can spot trends. Make them, even. I guess you could say that's what advertising and venture capitalism have in common."

She took a sip of her wine. "How did you find out about my job?"

"Simple online search," he replied before quirk-

ing a brow. "I wanted to make sure you weren't lying this time."

A guilty look crossed her face.

It was too easy to bait her—though she showed
plenty of signs of fight in her, he thought with
respect.

"What else did you learn?"

As she turned to sit in a wicker chair, he did the same.

He watched her close her eyes and turn her head to
the warm ocean breeze.

"Your tastes tend toward romantic tunes. Celine
Dion, Natalie Cole and Alicia Keys."

She opened her eyes and looked at him. "You
learned *that* from an Internet search?"

"No," he admitted. "From the favorites list on your
iPod. I took a look while you were out earlier."

"Payback?"

"Just curious."

And he meant it, he discovered. He wasn't gratu-
itously snooping. He was genuinely curious about her.
Hungry for details about who she was. The real woman
behind the masquerade.

"What else have you learned?"

"You live in London. You have an older brother
named Andrew who is a trader at Schroders, the British
investment firm. And two parents, Eleanor and George,
who own their own party-supply business."

"Very good," she murmured.

He sipped his wine. "Courtesy of local news articles
in the aftermath of Marie's death."

"That's what I would have expected."

"You have a preference for MAC cosmetics, French cheeses and Stella McCartney tops."

"Only her budget line," she replied. "Especially in my recent incarnation as a housekeeper."

"We'll get you the designer duds, I promise."

As he expected, she went straight for the bait.

"You've done more than enough shopping for me already. Thank you."

"You're welcome, but the offer still stands."

Her lips compressed.

"You attended Woldingham School and then read English Language & Communication at King's College London," he continued unperturbed.

He'd gotten her *curriculum vitae* from the Winter & Baker web site.

"So sorry the names are not as tony as Choate or Princeton," she returned. "Even so, I hope my qualifications suffice for the job of mistress."

His lips quirked. "They'll do."

"What a relief."

This time he let himself grin. "You should know I don't find sarcasm a turnoff."

"You forgot I like to ski," she replied, ignoring the loaded comment. "I've been to the Swiss Alps several times."

"Great. Then you should feel right at home in Vail. I have a lodge there."

"I know," she said with dry humor.

He cocked an eyebrow, and a shared moment of reluctant amusement passed between them.

"You're a fine cook…and a rotten housekeeper."

"I was otherwise occupied," she said.

This time it was his turn to say, "I know."

Their gazes held for a moment, before he turned and looked out past the terrace's rail.

He nodded in front of them, and then glanced back at her. "The sun is about to go down."

"Yes."

He watched as her eyes lowered and she breathed in deep of the ocean air, a smile curving her lips.

"Like it here?" he asked.

She turned to look at him. "It's beautiful. Peaceful."

He was glad she liked Bermuda. He was a fan of the place himself—blue, blue ocean and the endless vista of sky. And now she added to the beauty of it. For him.

"I saw you wandering the grounds earlier," he observed.

"It's an impressive house."

"The perfect location," he countered.

He'd seen the place and bought it, lured by the privacy and tranquility and location on one of Bermuda's best beaches.

The estate boasted its own pool, tennis court, guest and staff cottage, and landscaped gardens.

Jacinda turned to look at the sun's last rays, and Gage studied her face, the setting sun giving it a warm glow.

She truly was beautiful. Her classic features were smooth and relaxed, her curly brown hair loose and down around her shoulders. Her green eyes were rendered even paler by the reflected light of the sun and were fringed by thick, dark lashes.

She was suited to be *in* an ad as well as *creating* one.

But though she'd accused him of wanting to purchase her like an art object to add to his menagerie of beautiful things, the truth was he wanted to possess both her body and soul.

He looked out over the water.

They sat in silence, watching the sun disappear over the horizon, with the ocean's lapping waves as its parting gesture.

When the light had almost completely receded, leaving stillness behind, Gage looked down at his glass and then over at Jacinda's.

They'd both finished their wine, a damn fine Chardonnay.

But more importantly, the wine should have relaxed her. And judging by the companionable silence, it had worked.

Still, he wanted her.

He stood.

"Come on," he said, reaching for the wine bottle with the hand that wasn't holding his empty glass. "It's almost time for dinner."

She looked up at him blankly for a moment and then stood, apparently roused from her thoughts.

He stepped to one side, and she slid by him to enter the suite.

Once inside, he placed the wine bottle and glass down on the table she'd used for her own glass.

She was peering at the time on the bedside clock when he walked up behind her.

He cupped her upper arms and placed a kiss on her bare shoulder.

"We have to make sure you get some sun on this trip," he murmured.

She stilled. "In what?" she said, her voice coming out breathy. "The skimpy bikini I found among the purchases waiting for me?"

"There's a skimpy bikini?" he asked. "What color?"

"Emerald green, if you must know."

"Mmm," he replied, his voice laced with humor. "Remind me to give the staff a special bonus."

He nuzzled her neck, the shell of her ear and the tendrils of hair at her scalp.

"I thought you said it's time for dinner," she said huskily.

"Almost time," he corrected. "I wouldn't mind a little prelude first."

"Don't you mean interlude, as in 'romantic inter-lude'?" she replied as his hands went to the knot holding up her halter-top.

"Both."

The top fell away from her, and his hands came up to cup her bare breasts.

He kneaded, fueling his arousal.

When he circled over the peaks of her breasts, she moaned and slumped against him. She reached back and grasped his muscled thigh for support.

"Ah, Jacinda," he said in a low voice. "We may not trust or even like each other, but we always have this, don't we, sweetheart?"

She wet her lips. "I don't know what you mean."

He flicked his tongue over the shell of her ear and bit down lightly on her earlobe. "Liar. I think you do."

In the next instant, he turned her in his arms and pushed her back against the wall behind her, his mouth coming down on hers.

Her breasts pressed into his shirt, her dress held up below her chest by the zipper on her lower back.

She moaned again as his tongue swept inside her mouth, her arms sliding around his neck.

He pulled up the skirt of her dress so that it bunched at her hips, and one hand slid up her soft thigh.

She smelled of flowers and sun and surf. And she was making him crazy.

Pushing her panties aside, he parted her moist folds and delved into her waiting heat, stroking her.

Lifting his head, he watched her lips part and her eyes cloud as she gazed back at him.

"Let me fill you," he said deeply.

"That was the deal," she responded, her voice throaty.

He stilled for a second.

What had he expected? They *did* have a deal. She'd agreed to become his mistress.

But damn, her business-like response irked him.

He wanted to engage her mind, her emotions and her deepest fantasies.

He wanted her complete and utter capitulation, deal or no deal.

Aloud, he said, "That's right, sweetheart." He circled over her nerve center, making her gasp. "And I want you to enjoy it as much as I intend to."

"Gage." She moved restlessly against him.

"Ah, Jacinda, let it go," he coaxed.

There was nothing more erotic for him at the moment than having her come apart in his arms.

He pressed, swirled and then pushed inside her, flicking his thumb over her core, leaving them both breathless with want and pulsating need.

Her hands moved down to dig into his arms.

"Gage…"

"Yes?"

And then he watched with pleasure as she arched her back and came apart for him with a low moan.

Moments later, he kissed her softly. "I think I got my answer," he said in a low voice.

He stepped back and his fingers went to work on the buttons of his shirt, his need for her overwhelming him.

As they both undressed, they kissed again, repeatedly and with increasing desperation.

When they'd both shed their clothes, he sat back on the bed, drawing her to stand in front of him.

Then he leaned over to the night table and pulled out the foil packet he knew was there.

But before he could open it, she took it from him.

His eyes closed with pleasure as she sheathed him.

He leaned back then, taking her with him, so that she sat astride him.

He caught the look of surprise in her eyes.

"Aren't we ever going to have sex the traditional way?" she asked.

"What? Plain vanilla sex?" he asked. "Not if I can help it."

He positioned her and himself, and then watched

her shudder as she slid down over him. He savored the sensation as much as she did.

"Move for me, Jacinda," he murmured, before he lost his mind in a tidal wave of lust and desire unlike anything he'd felt with anybody else.

She moved, sinking down on him again and again, and his mouth closed over one breast, urging her on.

Their pants and gasps filled the otherwise silent room.

He turned his attention to the other breast, determined to take her with him when he came.

Their movements became more urgent.

And then suddenly he felt her squeeze around him. "Oh, Gage."

Her climax claimed her, and she shuddered.

His hands sank deep into her hips, and he raised up, pumping into her.

A second later, with a hoarse groan, he followed her over the edge.

Six

The next morning, Jacinda was forced to come to terms with her new status.

Billionaire's mistress.

She'd slept with Gage and was officially a kept woman in every sense.

She ought to be appalled, and she tried hard to summon the appropriate amount of outrage.

But the truth was she'd enjoyed going to bed with Gage.

The first time hadn't been a fluke. He was a wonderful lover, and last night again they'd been like a match set to parched wood.

She looked over at him, lounging next to her on a deck chair beside the pool, scanning a fax that had come through that morning.

Minutes before, he'd spread sunscreen on her back, and it was all she could do not to purr from the effect of his hands smoothing over her skin as he murmured his approval of her emerald-green bikini, his voice smoky with promise.

She was still recovering from the result of his touch, trying to keep her mind off of his smoothly muscled body laid out before her and the memory of running her fingertips over his back with sunscreen.

He, on the other hand, had apparently switched to work mode without missing a beat.

How was it possible, she wondered, for one man to revert from impassioned lover to cool corporate titan so easily?

Gage had said he'd had a taste of betrayal. Could that at least partly explain his guardedness, his ability to close up so quickly?

Curiosity overtook her. "It's occurred to me…"

He glanced up inquiringly.

"It's occurred to me," she started again, "that while I was pretending to be someone I'm not, you're actually the master of disguise."

He put down his fax. His eyes were still shielded by sunglasses, as were hers, but she could tell she had his complete attention now.

"And how do you figure that?" he asked.

"You hold your cards close to your chest."

"Some people call that a business asset."

"You're enigmatic," she tried again.

"That's all you can come up with after months of

snooping?" he teased, his tone gently mocking. "I'm disappointed."

"Guarded, I should have said."

"Most blackmailed billionaires are."

She shook her head. "I think it goes back further than that. You said you've tasted betrayal."

He sobered. "That's right. You could say I've had trouble with deceptive women before your recent acting routine."

"Your ex-wife?"

His lips twisted mirthlessly. "She came up on the Internet search, did she?"

"Google is an amazing thing."

"I should have figured."

"I hear the founders are billionaires today."

"And betraying the fraternity by giving up personal info on the other club members," he said with affected mournfulness.

"Too bad for you."

"I'm even more sorry I didn't get the chance to bankroll them when they got started," he responded, making her smile.

He sat back, his expression turning glib. "So what information about the redoubtable Mrs. Gage Lattimer would you like to know?"

"You divorced after less than two years of marriage." She made it a statement, but with an implicit invitation to elaborate.

"Yes, and that was eight years ago." The corner of his mouth turned up. "Back when I was a mere millionaire but still considered a good catch."

"No doubt."

"The trouble was I was also too love-struck to think about asking for a prenup when I met Roxanne," he continued. "She was an aspiring singer looking for her big break. I realized too late she thought her big break was me."

Ouch, Jacinda thought.

"When she asked for a divorce a year later and tried to take me to the cleaners, my divorce lawyer did some checking." Gage paused. "It turned out she'd hidden some interesting details about her background."

A weird premonition coiled in Jacinda's stomach.

"Credit card fraud coupled with a pattern of chasing men with money," Gage went on. "In other words, she was what some might label a 'gold digger'. Unfortunately for her, that little characteristic lowered the divorce settlement a bit."

"But you've done well for yourself since then," she offered.

"I haven't acquired any more wives," he replied, tongue-in-cheek.

"She must be sorry she didn't stay since you're a billionaire today."

"Maybe," he conceded, "but at the time, she had bigger fish to fry. I was her entrée into society, but once she was there, she didn't need me anymore. Divorcing me meant she was free to pursue rich types who had the same priorities—hitting the party circuit and keeping tabs on their social standing."

"I see."

The trouble was she *did* see, and all too well. Albeit belatedly.

With her masquerade, she'd hit a sore spot with Gage.

No wonder he'd been so furious when he'd discovered her subterfuge. In his eyes, she was another woman who'd approached him under false pretenses. But instead of being after his money, she'd been after information.

It must have taken something for someone like Gage, raised by formal and distant parents, to open up to another person. After his ex-wife betrayed him, he must have withdrawn again.

Gage only propositioning her to become his mistress suddenly made sense, Jacinda thought. He'd already learned to be guarded and cynical.

"So when you discovered I'd tricked you," she ventured, drawing her conclusion aloud, "you decided to punish me."

He quirked a brow. "Did last night feel like punishment?"

She felt herself heat up.

"Since we're on the subject, let's talk about the person who's influenced *your* life. Your sister."

The topic of Marie made her smile sadly. "My sister was impulsive…but always full of energy. She came along when I was four, and she was a dynamo from day one."

He tilted his head, regarding her. "You look alike. I should have seen the resemblance right off the bat. The curly brown hair, the big green eyes."

She shifted, feeling a ripple of awareness under his

scrutiny, and then nodded. "Yes, except Marie was a couple of inches shorter than I am."

"And you've always been the responsible older sister."

"Sedate, boring," she said with a laugh.

"Not in bed."

She could just make out his eyes behind his sunglasses at that moment, and they held hers.

She sighed. "I couldn't believe Marie was having a secret affair—one she didn't even tell *me* about."

"She must have had her reasons."

"And I'm afraid those reasons are why she wound up dead."

He nodded.

"Do you understand why I need to find out who this man is?" she asked. "Will you help me?"

"I said I would."

She drew in a breath, and then because there didn't seem to be anything else to say, she nodded at his fax. "Anything interesting with work?"

He glanced down, too. "Just a company I'm involved with. They need some marketing help, badly, at this point."

She pasted on a winning smile, lightening the mood. "Try me. I'm good with slogans."

He laughed. "Got anything that rhymes with Mandew? It's the founder's last name, and they're a computer start-up."

"'Can-do Mandew, We Do Great Things for You?'"

He laughed again. "Not bad for an on-the-spot idea. I see the beginnings of a great partnership."

Jacinda's breath caught.

Just what type of partnership they would have
remained to be seen, she thought, but their relationship
was getting more complicated by the day.

By the time they got back to New York, Gage was
feeling more relaxed than he'd been in ages.

A getaway with Jacinda to his Bermudan hideaway
had been just the ticket to rejuvenate him. He'd won a
game of tennis but she'd made him work for it, and
they'd also found time to go sailing and waterskiing. As
for the last, he'd been tempted to say the hell with it,
lay her on the floor of the power boat and make passionate love to her while the sun's rays beat down on them.

At night, they'd dined by moonlight and gone into
town for music and dancing. And of course, they'd ended
up in bed for more passionate bouts of lovemaking.

Along the way, he'd learned some interesting things
about Jacinda. Like him, she enjoyed challenging
herself with crossword puzzles. She was funny, especially when cornered, and smart as a whip. She could
talk about anything from world affairs to the latest
health topics knowledgeably.

They'd arrived back in New York late last night, in
time for the start of the weekend.

Now, Gage poured himself a cup of coffee in the
kitchen and took a sip, waiting for Jacinda to finish
getting showered and dressed and come down the stairs.

As he studied the Christmas decorations she had put
up, a smile played at his lips.

Maybe tonight he would whisk her to Radio City
Music Hall for the annual holiday show. He could get

one of his assistants to scrounge up tickets for good seats, or instead they could catch a Broadway show.

Jacinda might like either. He wondered whether she'd ever been to the city during the holidays, and somehow he doubted it.

This afternoon, they could do some holiday shopping. Barneys, Bergdorf and Tiffany all came to mind.

Gage smiled. He could picture how much Jacinda would protest if he bought her a bauble from a famed jeweler, and somehow he relished her reaction. He was enjoying getting a rise out of her these days—almost too much.

Still, since her secret was out, there was no longer any reason for her to hide her light under a bushel by dressing like a maid for his sake.

He could get used to keeping a mistress, Gage thought. Except right now the only woman he could picture in the role was Jacinda.

But he wasn't attracted only to her body. She had a fine mind—cagey but fine. She'd been smart enough to maintain a masquerade that had had him fooled for more than five months.

She challenged him, intrigued him and made him want her all the more.

The sound of footsteps roused him from his reverie.

When Jacinda came into view, he noticed she was wearing one of those pairs of jeans that had driven him crazy the past few months. They hugged all her curves and were paired with a fitted wraparound top in a burnt orange color. Black leather boots completed her ensemble.

Her hair was down and loose. He'd noticed she was wearing it that way now and was glad.

"Hi," he said. "Coffee?"

"Yes, please."

He reached for a new mug. "I was thinking about what we could do today. I thought you might like to do some holiday shopping." He poured some coffee into the mug. "Okay, if we start at Tiffany?"

He watched as she frowned.

Here we go, he thought with a hidden smile.

"Actually, I thought we'd go to Marie's apartment."

His humor faded. When he'd thought about possible itineraries for today, one thing that had never occurred to him was scouring Marie Endicott's old apartment.

"And why would we do that?" he asked without inflection.

She shrugged. "The apartment is still filled with Marie's things. I know it sounds batty but—" she shrugged again "—I thought we could take another look, in case there's something that's been overlooked the past few months."

"You know the police have been in there."

She nodded. "And so have I, but—"

He put the mug on the counter rather than hand it to her. "Jacinda, let the police do their job."

Her chin set at a stubborn angle. "You said you'd help me."

"And I have. I've leaned on the police."

"But the case remains unsolved."

"Right," he replied. "And there could be a murderer on the loose. You don't need to be taking risks."

The thought of Jacinda exposing herself to danger made him tense.

"How is it dangerous to visit my sister's old apartment?"

"If the crime was an inside job, and the police now think it was, someone in the building is dangerous. If he knows you're snooping, he could get nervous."

Her lips compressed, and he read mutiny in her expression. "I've been discreet."

"Nobody's seen you entering or leaving Marie's apartment?"

"No one," she confirmed, and then hesitated. "Well, except for once, when Amanda Crawford was in the elevator when I hopped in on the sixth floor."

He quirked an eyebrow. "My point exactly."

She looked exasperated. "You don't believe Amanda—"

"No, but someone at another time may have seen or heard you without your being aware of it."

She turned on her heel. "I'm going with or without you."

He trotted around the counter and took her arm. "Then it's with me. But at least let's have breakfast first."

He was never outmaneuvered, but she'd boxed him in. He wasn't going to let her go to Marie's apartment alone, not given what he knew about the crimes in the building.

She relaxed under his grasp. "I'll get breakfast."

"No, I will," he responded, smiling at her look of surprise. "I can make a mean cheese omelet."

"This I have to see."

"I've kept my culinary prowess a secret until now," he joked, "because I enjoyed having you cook for me."

"I should have guessed."

An hour later, after a delicious breakfast, they both slipped into Marie's apartment.

Gage walked around the space, taking in his surroundings.

The apartment was decorated in bright, cheery colors and comfortable furniture. A tidy kitchen was near the front door and was followed by a good-size living room. On either side of the living room were two bedrooms, one with a queen-size bed that had apparently been where Marie had slept, and the other with a smaller double bed presumably for overnight guests.

The two-bedroom apartment resembled a cozy bachelorette pad. But though the furniture and personal possessions were all there, someone had made some inroads in packing things up. Open and half filled cardboard boxes lay on a number of surfaces.

Pausing beside one box in Marie's bedroom, Gage noticed a framed photo lying on top of the packed contents. He pulled it out and studied it.

Marie and Jacinda smiled into the camera. Young and carefree, they had their arms around each other.

Jacinda came up beside him.

"That was taken while on holiday in the Canary Islands."

"You were obviously close," Gage remarked.

Jacinda nodded, and when he glanced at her, Gage noticed tears in her eyes.

Damn it.

Another reason why he hadn't wanted to come down here. He knew it would upset her.

"Let's get the job done," he said gruffly.

Jacinda nodded around them. "Just look through things, and pick up anything that seems interesting. You're a fresh pair of eyes. You might spot something the rest of us have missed."

He looked at the empty surface of a nearby desk. "My first inclination would be to start with electronic stuff, like e-mails and computer files. But I assume the police have their hands on it now?"

"Yes," Jacinda confirmed. "I know from Andrew that they came and took Marie's computer and cell phone once the investigation turned to possible murder. I've been left with packing up personal possessions."

She shrugged. "It's not much, but I don't want to leave any stone unturned."

"Okay then, why don't I look through stuff while I help you pack?" he said, making his tone comforting and upbeat. "I'll start in the living room, and you can work in here. Deal?"

Jacinda nodded.

Gage doubted they'd find anything interesting, but a deal was a deal.

With that thought, he went back into the living room, grabbed an empty box and started toward the built-in bookshelves along one wall.

Bookshelves, he thought, were the perfect place for tucking away slips of paper and other interesting stuff.

Half an hour later, though, he wasn't feeling nearly as sanguine.

He'd gleaned that Marie's reading tastes ran to popular fiction, real estate and some classics. But he hadn't discovered much else.

After tucking a couple of paperbacks into a cardboard box, he grabbed the next item on the shelf—a leather-bound copy of *Wuthering Heights*.

His lips quirked. According to family lore, his mother had, at one point, wanted to name him Heathcliff—or Heath, for short.

With idle curiosity, he opened the book and thumbed through the pages.

And then froze.

Instead of page after page of printed type, the book was filled with handwritten and dated entries in a feminine hand.

It seemed to be a diary. Marie's diary.

He swore under his breath.

Jacinda poked her head out of the bedroom. "Did you say something?"

He looked up, and the blank look on his face must have told her something because she walked over to him.

"What are you looking at?" she asked, looking down at the book in his hands.

He watched as her eyes widened.

"I think it's your sister's diary," he said.

Jacinda shook her head disbelievingly. "I didn't even know she kept one."

"Not only did she keep one," he said, flipping the volume closed, "but she took the trouble of hiding it in what looks from the outside like a leather-bound copy of *Wuthering Heights*."

Jacinda sucked in a breath, and then her eyes welled.

"Oh, Marie," she murmured. "Why all the subter-fuge?"

"We have to turn this over to the police."

"Not before we read it!"

"Jacinda…" he began warningly.

"Not here," she replied more urgently. "Upstairs in your apartment. We'll need to call the police and hand it over. But before that, we have time."

Seven

The minute they got back to Gage's apartment, Jacinda flopped down on the sofa and opened the volume in her hands.

"The first entry is from early last year," she said, aware of Gage sitting down next to her. "I'd recognize Marie's handwriting anywhere!"

Hungrily, she scanned the first page, which was filled with details about a night partying at the Lime-light. Still, nothing too revealing.

Even so, Jacinda felt a nervous tension grip her, as if she might burst out of her skin.

They might have found the key to Marie's death!

She couldn't believe it, and fought a tremor in her hands.

She flipped to the next page and the next and the next.

She couldn't seem to skim the pages fast enough, so she jumped to the end of the volume.

The last entry was from two days before Marie's death. It contained some ho-hum details about one of her potential real estate deals.

Frustrated, Jacinda turned the book so it opened at an early entry and flipped pages several at a time.

…visited the Met…

…bought fabulous dress at Saks…

…thinking of moving to larger apartment…

…called home today…spoke with Jacinda…

Seeing a reference to herself in her sister's hand gave her a pang. Oh, Marie.

She turned pages rapidly…until Gage reached out and stilled her hands.

"Jacinda," he said, "this isn't doing anyone any good. You're overwrought."

She pulled her hands out of his grasp, and then shot him a mutinous look. "I have to!"

After a moment, he sighed, apparently prepared to let her quest run its course.

She stared back down at the diary and continued to flip pages.

September 6th—I'll have to call him Ted because I don't dare write his real name even here.

Jacinda froze. Ted must have been Marie's secret lover.

At her sudden stillness, Gage leaned in and read over her shoulder.

As her finger traced down the page, she felt Gage go immobile, too.

Our tryst was at one of NYC's premier hotels.

He has the manners of another era, unlike most of the men I meet. And great in bed!

I knew it was wrong. He's married. But I couldn't help myself.

Jacinda felt her stomach plummet as if in free fall.

Her sister had been having an affair with a married man. A rich and powerful *married* man.

No wonder her sister had been so secretive.

And it may have cost her her life.

Oh, Marie.

"Marie was having an affair with a married man," she said in a choked voice, as if saying it aloud would make it easier to believe.

"I know," Gage said quietly. "I was reading along with you."

She looked up at Gage in anguish. "Why didn't she tell me?"

"I'm sure she didn't want to disappoint you."

Sympathy, kindness even, was etched on Gage's face. If she hadn't been so shocked and distraught, she would have marveled at this latest glimpse of the man behind the master-of-the-universe facade.

She nodded at him but emotion welled up anyway, refusing to be kept at bay.

As sobs wracked her, Gage removed the diary from her hands and pulled her into his arms.

"Go ahead and cry," he murmured. "You've been strong and brave."

She burrowed her head into his shoulder, and he rubbed her back.

She'd thought she'd shed all the tears she was capable of over her sister's death, but this latest shocker had sent her reeling, stripping her of her defenses and leaving her vulnerable.

How ironic, she realized amidst her jumbled thoughts, that she was being comforted by the man she'd once suspected of being responsible for Marie's death.

But there was no other place she'd rather be right now than in the shelter of Gage's arms. There was a haven there that was both unexpected and welcome.

Jacinda put her head down against a strong wind blowing along Park Avenue as she headed toward number 721.

Soon after her crying fit yesterday, Gage had called Detective McGray of the NYPD, and then she and Gage had gone over to the police precinct together.

Gage had introduced himself and then her as Marie's sister. From the look on Detective McGray's face, it was obvious he was surprised to see them together.

Without further elaboration, she had explained that she'd been packing up things in her sister's apartment and Gage had been helping her.

The detective's surprise had soon been replaced by interest in their new find. Marie's diary.

Detective McGray had absorbed the news that they now had solid evidence of Marie's secret affair with an impassive expression.

But with a glance at Gage, he had promised to do all he could to crack the case.

Jacinda dug her fingernails into her palms.

She'd been right, and the police had been wrong.

Now, as she turned under the green awning of 721 Park Avenue and stepped into the building lobby, Jacinda noted absently that there wasn't a doorman in sight.

Crossing the lobby to the elevator bank, however, she heard voices coming from the mail room.

And from the tone of those voices, it sounded like two people were arguing.

She slowed and then, because she couldn't help being curious, she stopped once she reached the doorman's wide mahogany desk.

Her footsteps had been muffled by the Oriental rug covering the center of the ivory marble floor, and judging by the steady staccato sound of the voices, it seemed neither party in the mail room was aware of her presence.

The sound of the disagreement was startling. No one argued, not even in a furious whisper, in 721's lobby, which reeked of wealth, luxury and hush-hush class.

And she couldn't be sure, but it sounded like the voices belonged to Henry Brown and Vivian Vannick-Smythe.

Jacinda wondered what Vivian was complaining about, and she only marveled that Henry was responding. Perhaps Henry had been in his job long enough that he didn't fear the wrath of the building's icy matron.

She strained to catch a word, but after several moments without being able to make out anything, she relaxed.

She was eavesdropping, and she really ought to move on.

In the next moment, however, instead of proceeding toward the elevator bank, she found herself tiptoeing closer to the mail room entrance.

She'd taken four or five steps, however, when Vivian's voice reached her.

"…Marie Endicott…"

Jacinda froze.

Why would Vivian mention Marie's name during an argument with Henry?

She shook her head.

Were her ears playing tricks on her? Was she so desperate to solve the mystery of her sister's death after this many months that everything seemed somehow connected to Marie?

She heard a rustling sound, as if someone was moving about, and hurriedly decided to resume her stride.

She looked over her shoulder in time to see Henry Brown emerge from the mail room and frown when he saw her.

She gave the young dark-haired man a sunny smile.

"Hello," she called. "Cold today."

"We'll get some snowflakes tomorrow," he responded, his expression clearing but still not cracking a smile.

A second later, one of Vivian's shih tzus appeared at Henry's side and started barking.

"So I've heard," she responded over the dog's barks, and then hurried forward to punch the button for the elevator.

From the corner of her eye, she noticed Henry making a production of shuffling some paper at the doorman's desk while the dog at his side growled at her.

She breathed a sigh of relief when the elevator arrived and she was able to step inside and bid *adieu* to the yapping ball of fur.

It was only when the doors closed, however, that she realized Vivian had yet to emerge from the mail room.

The minute she got upstairs, she called Gage at his office.

"Hi. Everything okay?" he said.

She took a deep breath. "Actually…"

"What's up?" Gage asked, his tone sharpening.

"I just came through the building lobby, and I heard Vivian Vannick-Smythe arguing with Henry Brown in hushed tones in the mail room."

"So?" Gage asked, his tone relaxing. "Vivian is grouchy enough to light into one of the building staff."

"I can't be sure, but I think I heard her mention Marie's name."

"And?"

"And I think Henry and Vivian may know something we don't about Marie's death."

After a moment, Gage's sigh was audible. "Jacinda, stop playing amateur sleuth. Just because Vivian mentioned Marie's name doesn't mean she had something to do with your sister's death. The whole building's been speculating about Marie's death off and on since it happened. Everyone knows the police are investigating."

"You don't believe me?" She felt a stab, as if Gage's opinion mattered more than most.

"You said yourself you couldn't be sure it was Marie's name that was mentioned."

"Have you noticed Vivian's dogs never bark at Henry?"

"No."

"I think those two have a connection they're hiding."

"Of course the dogs don't bark at Henry. He's the doorman. They see him all the time, and they recognize someone familiar."

"I think there's more to the story."

"Jacinda, stop it." He added with sudden suspicion, "Did anyone catch you eavesdropping?"

She hesitated. "Henry emerged from the mail room and spotted me heading toward the elevators."

She heard Gage swear under his breath.

"Jacinda, for the last time, let the police do their job."

"And I do mine?" she retorted. "Namely, taking care of you?"

"That's not what I meant."

"Then what did you mean?"

"We recently found Marie's diary, and you're eager for more leads. But let the police investigation run its course, and don't let your imagination take flight in the meantime."

He sounded so reasonable, so convincing, so sure.

Perhaps Gage was right, Jacinda thought.

After all, her instincts had already been proven wrong once—when she'd thought *he'd* been responsible for Marie's death.

Since then, she'd done a complete about-face. In fact, these days, more than anything, she feared falling in love with him.

"Sit tight until I get home," Gage said.

She sighed, and then responded reluctantly, "Okay."

"Oh, and Jacinda?"

"Yes?"

"I may be home a little later than usual."

"Right, okay," she answered.

After ending the call, Jacinda looked around the penthouse.

She'd find something to do with herself. What was a mistress supposed to do with her time?

Shop? Do lunch? Avail herself of the chauffeured car that Gage had put at her disposal?

She didn't know anyone well enough to invite to lunch. Elizabeth Wellington next door seemed quite nice, and she knew Gage was friends with Elizabeth's husband, but Elizabeth had her hands full with a baby these days. Besides, no one knew she'd morphed from being Gage's housekeeper to his lover, and it would look odd for Gage's maid to be issuing invitations to lunch.

And as far as shopping, what would she do? Go looking for a tiara and gown? Those were for a princess, not a mistress.

Of course, the one thing she was itching to do was solve the mystery of her sister's death.

Maybe she could take a stroll. And so what if her meanderings happened to take her to the door of the police station?

What could it hurt to mention to Detective McGray what she'd overheard?

Wouldn't the police appreciate all the leads they could get, even if some of them ultimately proved false?

She'd told Gage she'd sit tight, but that didn't mean a stroll around the neighborhood wasn't in the cards.

After the call with Jacinda, Gage stared at his office phone for a few moments.

Making up his mind, he picked up the receiver and dialed the number he'd taken down two weeks ago.

"McGray here," a gravelly voice announced.

"It's Gage Lattimer."

"How can I help you?" the detective said, sounding more alert.

"Jacinda Endicott just overheard an argument in the building lobby between one of the building residents, Vivian Vannick-Smythe, and one of our doormen, Henry Brown."

"Yeah?"

"The argument apparently involved Marie Endicott," Gage elaborated.

"Interesting."

"I think so, too," Gage replied blandly.

"Might be time for another chat with Mrs. Vannick-Smythe and Henry Brown."

"Maybe so," Gage agreed. "And, Detective?"

"Yes?"

"If you do find anything interesting, I'd appreciate your letting me know ASAP. I'm in touch with Jacinda Endicott."

Not only that, I'm sleeping with her.

"Will do," McGray responded before they ended their call.

After replacing the receiver, Gage stared at the phone thoughtfully.

The lead might not go anywhere. On the other hand, it just might.

Eight

It was a bittersweet Christmas Eve.

Her first without Marie. Her first with Gage.

Jacinda sprinkled pine nuts on the fillet of sole on the kitchen counter in front of her.

When it had become clear Gage would be spending Christmas by himself in New York, Jacinda had made up her mind to stay, as well.

It wasn't that Gage had demanded she remain in New York. But Jacinda told herself that with recent breaks in Marie's case, she couldn't afford to leave town.

Of course, the more complicated story, which she refused to fully acknowledge to herself, was that Gage himself was a draw to remaining in New York.

She enjoyed his company, and she was powerfully attracted to him.

Under other circumstances, she would have been ecstatic at meeting a man like Gage. But she was his temporary bargained-for mistress until Marie's case was solved.

She steeled herself for that day, because while Gage had shown every sign of enjoying their affair, Jacinda knew he'd been burned in the past. And she didn't kid herself that Gage had forgotten she was another woman who'd come into his life with a hidden ulterior motive.

She sighed as she dusted pine nut crumbs from her hands.

Mouth-watering aromas filled the penthouse from her baking and cooking, and the sounds of a Christmas medley floated in the background.

The cooking was a way to channel her restless energy, because no matter how much progress had been made, there remained a big question mark next to Marie's death.

Jacinda knew her family hadn't been too happy when she'd announced she was staying across the Atlantic for the holidays. They'd sounded worried, too, as if they were concerned she continued to be consumed by grief. Jacinda hadn't wanted to raise false hopes by telling them of recent breaks in the case, namely, the discovery of Marie's diary, and perhaps the conversation between Vivian and Henry.

Because her family had appeared not to know of the diary, she assumed Detective McGray had trusted her to pass along the information.

At the thought of Detective McGray, she recalled when she'd stopped by his office the other day.

He had been dismissive of the argument between Vivian and Henry, just as Gage had.

Miffed but willing to hold her tongue in the interest of keeping the police's cooperation, she'd accepted the detective's opinion with outward equanimity.

But privately, she still found herself clinging to the belief that something important had transpired in the conversation between Vivian Vannick-Smythe and Henry Brown.

So, here she was trying to direct her energies toward something positive, preparing meals that would make a *chef de cuisine* proud.

Tomorrow, she'd present a traditional English Christmas dinner. Roast turkey with stuffing, roast potatoes and bread sauce. Also, parsnips and swede, Brussels sprouts and chestnuts. And of course, the traditional Christmas fruit pudding, which she'd prepared weeks ago, even before it had become clear she and Gage would be spending Christmas together in New York.

But tonight, she reflected, she and Gage would dine on lighter fare. A delicately prepared fillet of sole with pine nuts and chives. A side of asparagus tips and seasoned couscous.

She was just sliding the prepared sole into Gage's top-of-the-line sub-zero refrigerator when voices reached her from the front door.

She turned around in surprise, but before she could react, Gage stepped inside, followed by Detective McGray of the New York Police Department.

Gage looked grim, and Jacinda tensed.

This could not be good news on Christmas Eve.

Minutes ago Gage had gone down to the lobby to retrieve the mail.

Now, he halted and nodded over his shoulder. "Jacinda, you know Detective McGray. He was walking into the lobby when I got downstairs."

She walked out of the kitchen. "Detective McGray."

"Ms. Endicott," the detective said gruffly with a nod of his head.

If Detective McGray thought it was odd he'd found her cooking in Gage's kitchen, he didn't remark on it.

"May I take your coat?" she asked.

It was ridiculous. She knew the detective was here to discuss something momentous, but she felt as if she were having an out-of-body experience.

"I'll take care of the coat, Jacinda," Gage said as the detective shed his. "Why don't you and Detective McGray get seated?"

At her questioning look, Gage added, "There's been a break in the case."

She and Detective McGray walked over to sit on facing couches in the living room, and after dealing with the detective's coat, Gage came to sit down next to her.

Not for the first time, Jacinda noted Detective McGray looked like any other overworked and underpaid veteran of the NYPD.

"Ms. Endicott, earlier today we arrested Senator Michael Kendrick for the murder of your sister," the detective said without preamble.

Jacinda felt as if someone had knocked the breath out of her. "What?"

"We've recovered the security camera videotape of the building roof from the night of your sister's death. It appears your sister and Senator Kendrick had some sort of altercation, and he pushed her to her death."

Jacinda sucked in a deep breath, and then felt tears sting the back of her eyes.

Finally. *Finally.* The truth was out.

Gage stroked her arm. "Are you okay?"

She nodded, momentarily unable to speak.

At last, she said, "How? You had a theory it was a building insider who was behind the crime."

"You didn't know?" Gage responded for the detective. "Kendrick lived in 8C with his wife until July. They moved out and put their co-op on the market."

Right when Marie died, Jacinda thought. And right before she assumed her persona as Jane Elliott.

"We've got evidence the senator was romantically involved with your sister," Detective McGray said. "The senator's wife was aware her husband was cheating—though not with whom. That's probably why they separated. When we arrested the senator earlier today, Charmaine Kendrick came forward with love letters she'd discovered between her husband and his anonymous lover."

Jacinda frowned. "I'm surprised Senator Kendrick's wife was so willing to cooperate. She doesn't sound like the typical political wife."

"You've never met Charmaine, have you?" Gage

asked rhetorically, looking at her. "I got the feeling she was unhappy with Kendrick for a long time. And being the wronged wife, selling him out gives her more leverage in divorce proceedings."

Gage added dryly, "And believe me, divorce is something I know a lot about."

"How did you find the building tape after all this time?" Jacinda asked Detective McGray.

"Vivian Vannick-Smythe produced it."

At Jacinda's look of surprise, Detective McGray cleared his throat. "Mrs. Vannick-Smythe in 12A and her lover, Henry Brown, have been blackmailing the residents of this building."

Jacinda gaped at the detective. "What? How did you discover that?"

It was a bombshell.

"When we questioned both Vivian and Henry about the happenings in the building," Detective McGray said, "they both initially denied any involvement."

Jacinda nodded. "Of course."

She couldn't imagine the icy matron on the twelfth floor conceding anything. Vivian Vannick-Smythe had probably bristled at even being accosted by the police.

Detective McGray looked cynical. "But Vivian got nervous once we told her we were also questioning Henry Brown at the station house. So she decided to cut a deal. Once she'd summoned her lawyer, of course."

"Let me guess," Gage said.

Detective McGray gave a curt nod. "She was willing

to cooperate once she'd gotten a guarantee we'd go easy on her."

"So she decided to sell out her lover," Jacinda concluded.

"You could say that," Detective McGray replied. "As far as we can make out by putting together Vivian's and Henry's stories, the truth is both of them were in on the blackmail schemes from the beginning. The videotape of the roof from the night of the murder was one thing they were using to blackmail Senator Kendrick. That's why they were holding on to it."

Jacinda's nails dug into the palms of her hands. Vivian Vannick-Smythe was a mean-spirited shrew.

To think how much she and her family had suffered these past several months while all along Vivian had held the key to solving her sister's murder!

"Vivian gave us the evidence to arrest Kendrick in exchange for our agreeing not to prosecute her for blackmail and withholding evidence," McGray said in a gravelly voice.

"And Henry caved and talked?" Gage asked.

Detective McGray shifted his gaze from Jacinda to Gage. "Only once we told him Vivian had fingered him as the perpetrator of the blackmails. He confessed he'd been Vivian's lover and that she'd convinced him to engage in the blackmail with her."

Jacinda felt a twinge of sympathy for Henry. He was on the hook for several felonies while Vivian would be let off easy for her cooperation. It must have been Henry who'd answered the phone back in July when she'd placed that fateful call from London seeking information about Gage's former housekeeper.

"You said the tape was *one* thing they were using to blackmail Kendrick," Gage pressed. "There's more?"

Jacinda looked at both men perplexedly. "Why? Why did he have to kill my sister? It doesn't make any sense."

"Unfortunately, it does," Detective McGray responded, a hint of sympathy entering his voice. "One possible motive for the killing is that Kendrick believed your sister was the one blackmailing him."

Jacinda sucked in a breath. The news sent her reeling.

"You see," Detective McGray elaborated, "Henry admitted he and Vivian initially blackmailed Kendrick by threatening to expose his extramarital affair and ruin his political career."

"And since Kendrick had been so careful, so discreet, about his affair with Marie," Gage guessed, "he must have figured Marie could be the only source of the blackmail letter."

"Exactly," Detective McGray said.

Jacinda shook her head in disbelief. "How did Vivian and Henry even discover the affair?" She looked at the detective. "You and I didn't find anything, and we both looked through Marie's things."

"Henry admitted he and Vivian snuck into the Kendricks' apartment when they lived in the building. My guess is they got hold of a love letter or two, like Mrs. Kendrick did."

"But why didn't we find any letters in Marie's apartment?"

McGray shrugged. "It's possible Kendrick destroyed them. After he was blackmailed and got nervous, he must have been inside Marie's apartment at some point and gotten his hands on them."

Jacinda shook her head again. "How could he and Marie be so discreet and yet leave love letters?"

McGray coughed. "The love notes were signed with pet names and must have been hand-delivered somehow, or at least hidden in places only the other party would know about."

"So Vivian and Henry knew Kendrick was having an extramarital affair with *someone*," Gage mused, "but they didn't realize with *whom* until they got hold of the videotape."

"That's probably right," McGray agreed. "Too bad for Kendrick he didn't realize the roof was being videotaped."

Jacinda perked up. "Has Kendrick confessed to killing my sister?"

McGray snorted with disdain. "Kendrick is a politician—and a powerful one. He hasn't admitted anything, but he's got a lawyer. This thing's going to blow big once it hits the papers. It's going to make Kendrick's problem with his staff and the ongoing SEC prosecution seem like small potatoes."

"I remember now that Marie mentioned she was volunteering with Senator Kendrick's reelection campaign," Jacinda mused out loud. "And of course, the two of them living in the same building provided the perfect cover."

It all made sense, she thought, why she and the police had been unable to find a paper or electronic trail from Marie to the senator. The two had lived in the same building, so there hadn't been any need for long-distance communication. All the senator had had to do was knock on Marie's door.

Jacinda recalled coming across Kendrick's reelection campaign material in her sister's apartment. It hadn't seemed remarkable at the time that Marie would be volunteering for the senator's reelection bid. And as a result, any calls from Marie to the senator's campaign office wouldn't have looked suspicious.

It must have been audacious and reckless for the senator to have both his wife and his mistress under the same roof. But also extremely convenient.

The evidence had been right under her nose, Jacinda thought.

Why hadn't she suspected anything? Had she been too naive to believe her sister could have an affair with a married man? A powerful elected official?

Oh, Marie.

"According to Henry Brown's confession," Detective McGray said, "Senator Kendrick was the only 721 Park Avenue resident to pay the blackmail money. Everyone else refused and went to the police."

"Kendrick is an idiot," Gage muttered.

Jacinda looked over at him. "More than an idiot. A murderer."

Now that the initial shock of discovering who had killed her sister had worn off, she felt the gates open on her pent-up frustration.

She'd waged a lonely battle for six months. Her initial hunch had been correct—her sister had been murdered. She'd been right, and the police had been wrong.

And rather than volunteering his assistance, Gage had offered her the role of mistress in exchange for his help.

"I'd like to see the videotape," she said thickly, addressing Detective McGray.

The detective hesitated. "Are you sure you're ready? And that you want to? We try to spare families the graphic details."

Jacinda raised her chin. "Tell me."

Detective McGray looked down and studied the rug. "Your sister and Kendrick appeared to be arguing," he said gruffly. "I'm assuming he lured her up to the roof with the promise of a lovers' tryst, but he intended to confront her about the blackmail. In any case, on the tape, Marie looks as if she's shaking her head in denial just before…"

The detective trailed off.

"Just before Kendrick pushed Marie off the roof," Jacinda finished, tears stinging the backs of her eyes.

No wonder Detective McGray thought Kendrick had assumed Marie was blackmailing him. The video-taped argument certainly supported that theory.

She looked from Gage to Detective McGray. "Everyone discouraged me, but I knew, *knew,* right from the beginning that my sister hadn't killed herself."

"Ms. Endicott," Detective McGray said, "I can understand why you're upset right now—"

"I've been upset for six months," she shot back, and

then stood. "Thank you for stopping by, Detective. I appreciate your coming here to tell me the news yourself."

Her tone was cold, impersonal.

After a momentary look of surprise, and after shooting a glance at Gage, the detective stood, too. Gage followed suit.

"I'm sorry for your loss, Ms. Endicott."

Jacinda nodded numbly.

"I'll show the detective out," Gage said.

"Thank you," she said to no one in particular, and then turned to walk toward the back of the penthouse.

She was done with the police—and with Gage.

"Are you all right?" Gage asked in the doorway to the master bedroom.

"Fine," she said, not looking up from gathering some toiletries into a case.

"You don't look okay."

In fact, she felt as if she'd gone nine rounds with a phantom opponent, Jacinda thought.

The fight was over, however. Marie's killer had finally been found.

But while she'd slowly been coming to terms with the loss of her sister over the past several months, now she was facing losing Gage, too.

Her heart ached.

Then she shook herself.

The twinge didn't make sense. She was mad at him.

He'd made her pay for his help. Then he'd dragged his feet, more interested in continuing their affair than in helping her solve a crime.

But now that Marie's case was solved, and their bargain was over, she wouldn't let him put her aside like another cast-off plaything. She'd protect herself by beating him to goodbye.

"It's late in London," she said, "but I'll need to call Andrew…my parents…"

"There's time for that," Gage replied.

"That's always been your philosophy, hasn't it?" she replied sharply.

Gage frowned. "Meaning?"

"Meaning you were never too keen on solving Marie's murder." She mimicked, "'Let's go to Bermuda, Jacinda. Let the police do their jobs, Jacinda.'"

Gage's brows snapped together.

"In fact, you were happy for the investigation to drag on as long as I continued as your mistress!"

Jacinda watched in satisfaction as Gage's scowl disappeared and his face went blank.

"You just wanted satisfaction—to continue punishing me for deceiving you!"

"Is that what you believe?"

"That's what I *know*," she said, zipping up her case and picking up her handbag from the bed. "Marie's case has been solved, so according to the terms of our bargain, our affair is over."

She headed toward the door.

"Where are you going?" Gage demanded.

"Home, to get my luggage and pack," she said without glancing at him. "If I hurry, I may even be able to get back to London before Christmas is over."

Tears threatened, but she held them back. "What a gift that would be!"

What an utterly depressing Christmas, all around, she thought.

Still, she kept walking, marching down the penthouse stairs, even as her lips quivered.

It was only when she got to the pavement outside, and raised her hand for a taxi instead of letting one of Henry Brown's fellow doormen do it for her, that she let the tears flow.

Nine

Damn it.

As soon as Gage heard the front door close behind Jacinda, he felt the strange silence of being alone on Christmas Eve in a city of upward of eight million people.

He was tempted to go after Jacinda, but he reined himself in.

She'd floored him with the accusation that he'd made halfhearted efforts to solve Marie's murder because he was content with her as his mistress.

His initial reaction had been to deny it, but then he'd caught himself.

He'd forced himself to confront motivations he'd previously been unwilling to stop and examine.

Jacinda's accusation was true. At least partly.

Gage raked his hand through his hair in frustration and looked around the master bedroom.

Jacinda had left her stamp on the room.

Some of her things lay about, and her scent still hung in the air.

Gage glanced at the bed and remembered the impassioned nights the two of them had spent there.

He'd found a release—no, a freedom—in her arms that he hadn't in any other woman's.

She was ambitious but warm—exactly what he was looking for.

She'd used stealth to infiltrate his life and slip past his defenses. But once inside his home, she'd become a part of his life he couldn't do without.

And now she was gone.

Our affair is over, she'd said.

It was true, he'd struck a bargain with her—one that he wasn't too proud of, in retrospect. And now that Kendrick had been arrested, there was no reason for Jacinda to stick around.

There was no way to get her to stay…unless, maybe, he put everything on the line.

It was time to let go of the past, Gage realized. To let go of the fact that their relationship had started on the wrong foot, with a crime followed by deceit and a devil's bargain. And even more, it was time for him to let go of baggage from his divorce that had helped sour his relationship with Jacinda.

Gage checked his watch. It was a few minutes after four.

If he hurried, he'd have time to pick up a new Christmas gift for Jacinda, and then get to her apartment before she left for the airport. He was betting it would take her some time to pack and contact an airline.

If necessary, though, he'd follow her to London.

He'd already picked out an expensive but tasteful gold watch for Jacinda, but he decided to save that gift for tomorrow. If he had tomorrow. Today he needed to pull out the works.

He was also betting his usual chauffeur would remember Jacinda's address. He'd had Jacinda use his car and driver in the past to run errands and pick up stuff from her studio apartment.

Striding out of the bedroom, he found his cell phone and called his driver, asking him to be ready immediately.

He grabbed his coat from the entry closet and, shrugging into it, opened the door of his apartment…and came face to face with the Wellingtons across the hall.

They turned to look at him in surprise. Elizabeth was holding Lucas, and Reed had his key in the door. They were obviously on their way in or out.

"Happy holidays, Gage!" Elizabeth said.

The holidays didn't seem so cheery to him at the moment, Gage thought, but he was hoping to fix the situation.

"Have you heard the news?" Reed asked. "We just got a call from the police."

So, Detective McGray and his fellow cops at the NYPD had wasted no time, Gage thought. News was spreading fast. It would break in the media soon—if it hadn't already.

"I've heard," Gage said shortly.

"Another reason to be thankful at the holidays," Elizabeth said as the baby waved his arms and chortled.

Reed looked at him more closely. "Anything wrong? Did the police call you?"

"In fact, I got a visit from Detective McGray himself."

Reed raised his eyebrows. "Surprising."

"Not really," Gage replied, "when your housekeeper happens to be Marie Endicott's sister."

Reed's face registered surprise, and Elizabeth's eyes widened.

Reed recovered first. "Crime solving in your spare time, were you?" he said with dry humor.

"I knew there was more to your relationship with Jacinda than met the eye!" Elizabeth exclaimed.

Gage leaned over and stabbed the button for the elevator. "At the moment, I've got to catch up with Jacinda before she boards a flight to London."

He straightened and belatedly took in the heart-warming domestic tableau that the Wellingtons presented. A happily married couple, one baby and another on the way.

This was what he could have. *This* was what he wanted. Suddenly, he saw his future.

If he hurried.

Reed eyed him. "Of course. Don't let us hold you up."

"Good luck!" Elizabeth called as the elevator doors opened and Gage stepped inside.

"Thanks," Gage shot back before the doors closed.

His driver arrived a few minutes after Gage got downstairs. And fortunately, his chauffeur remembered driving Jacinda to York Avenue and Eighty-second Street a couple of times to collect her belongings.

After they made a quick side trip to pick up Jacinda's gift, the driver headed toward York Avenue.

The going was slow, however, because rush hour had begun and there was significant holiday pedestrian traffic.

Gage thrummed his fingers on the leather-upholstered armrest of his seat.

When they arrived at Jacinda's apartment, he hopped out and cursed under his breath when he saw the building had a security camera but no doorman.

He looked at the doorbells and was relieved that the name Elliott was taped under the buzzer for Apt. 5B. It looked as if Jacinda had gone to some lengths to make her identity as Jane Elliott appear real, and for once, Gage was thankful for it.

He knew she wouldn't be inclined to let him upstairs, but he punched the buzzer anyway and waited.

When there was no answer, he tried again…and again.

Was she ignoring him? Or—dread slammed into him—was he too late and she'd already headed to the airport?

He was spared further debate, however, when a resident of the building happened by.

He smiled at the older man, and lying through his teeth, apologized for not being able to find his key.

The older man took one look at his expensive suit, and with a curt nod, held the door open, allowing Gage to follow him in.

As Gage rode the elevator up, he thanked the powers that be for unquestioning New Yorkers.

When he got to the fifth floor, he stopped in front of 5B and knocked.

When there was no answer, he glanced at the crack between the door and the floor.

No light. No sound.

Damn it.

She could swear there wasn't a free cab on the whole island of Manhattan at the moment.

Jacinda trudged along Eighty-second Street, pulling her wheeled suitcase behind her.

She was still in shock over everything that had transpired earlier in the day.

Senator Kendrick had been arrested for her sister's death.

Once she'd reached her studio apartment, she'd pulled up the senator's picture online. The minute she'd seen Kendrick's photo, everything had clicked for her. Kendrick was tall, dark-haired and dark-eyed. And he had a noticeable dimple.

Afterward, she'd called her parents in London to let them know Senator Kendrick had been arrested for Marie's murder.

The call had been an emotional wringer. She'd shed copious tears along with her mother, an ocean away.

At the end of the call, she'd told her parents she would try to get a stand-by seat on a flight to London, however much the odds were stacked against her.

One thing she hadn't counted on, though, was how difficult it would be to find a taxi to the airport.

On Christmas Eve, Manhattan was thronged with

tourists and shoppers. On top of it all, she was cold, miserable and getting more dispirited by the second.

Of course, she could try the airport shuttle train, or one of the buses that departed from Forty-second Street to the airport. But she'd have to take the subway to either of those, and the nearest subway stop was a long way from York and Eighty-second Street.

Still, she was starting to realize she might not have a choice.

Turning the corner of Eighty-second onto York, she looked up…and stopped short.

The breath went out of her.

Gage.

He was bent, leaning into the passenger side window of a black limo with tinted windows, apparently speaking with the driver.

She stood frozen in place as he straightened and looked up and down the street.

His eyes came to rest on her and he stilled.

Jacinda didn't think she could bear facing him again. Why was he here?

After a moment, Gage walked toward her, his face unreadable.

When he came to a stop, he looked down at her suitcase and then back up at her. "Need a ride?"

His offer was heaven-sent. Or not.

She lifted her chin. "I need to get to JFK."

"That's what I figured," he replied.

She eyed him warily.

"You won't catch a cab here."

"Are you going to force me to accept a ride from you just like you coerced me into becoming your mistress?" she retorted.

His jaw tightened and then relaxed. "I guess I deserved that."

His mea culpa took her by surprise.

He gestured to the car behind him. "However, the offer still stands."

She wavered, and then reluctantly moved toward him. "Since you're my only option, I accept."

When she drew near, he reached down and grasped the handle of her suitcase, stopping her progress.

"I'll get your luggage," he said.

She looked up at him, their faces inches apart, and swallowed. "Fine. Thank you."

There was nothing like having a billionaire help you with your luggage, Jacinda thought. Her girl-friends and coworkers back in London would think she was bonkers for leaving Gage behind.

Then she shook herself. She was not bonkers. He was a jerk, she thought, her resolution hardening.

After Gage had deposited her suitcase in the trunk of the car, he opened the car door for her and she got in, making herself comfortable in the plush leather-upholstered interior.

Gage came around and got in himself after a quick word to the driver.

After noting the privacy partition separating her from the driver and obscuring the view ahead, Jacinda decided her best course was to stare out the passenger window.

She watched the shoppers hurry along with bags of gifts, and her heart ached.

The whole world seemed to be happy—except for her.

"Jacinda."

"Hmm?"

"Look at me."

She turned her head around. "Is that an order?"

"It's a request."

"How generous of you."

"I know I hurt you."

Her lips parted. "Marie's death hurt me."

"I've been an ass."

"Well, points to you for being able to concede that much!"

"You should know, though, that I went to the police with your suspicions about Vivian and Henry."

His declaration surprised her. "You did?"

He nodded, and for the first time, she thought she detected a hint of vulnerability in Gage's face.

"Detective McGray was so dismissive of my suspicions when I told him," she said.

"Probably because it was old news to him by that point," Gage said. "I called him right after the call with you about Vivian and Henry."

"Oh." So Gage hadn't been completely dismissive of her suspicions.

"Henry admitted to the police that he and Vivian were having a disagreement over his cut of the senator's blackmail money," Gage went on. "Henry's deal with Vivian was for twenty-five percent of the money from the blackmail schemes, but when no one but the senator paid up, Henry thought he was entitled to more. That was the argument you heard in the mail room."

Gage added dryly, "I should have known you wouldn't listen to me and sit tight."

"Of course, and I was right to go to the police."

"You accused me of not being interested in solving Marie's death because I wanted to prolong our affair," Gage countered.

"Yes."

She felt herself flush because she knew now she'd been somewhat unfair in her accusation. "Why didn't you tell me you phoned Detective McGray? Why did you suggest I was letting my imagination get the better of me where Vivian and Henry were concerned?"

Gage sighed. "After thinking about it a little more, I realized the conversation you overheard was an angle worth pursuing. But I didn't want you putting yourself in danger. There was a murderer on the loose, and the police thought someone in the building was responsible."

"I see."

She felt a shiver of emotion shoot through her. Gage cared about her.

"And you were only partly right in your accusation," he said.

Catching the look in his eyes, Jacinda held her breath.

"I did want to prolong our affair, but not to continue punishing you," Gage said, looking deep into her eyes. "It was because I wanted you. I was falling for you."

Her lips parted.

"I'm in love with you, Jacinda."

Her heart thudded inside her at his words.

"I've been an ass, but I'll spend the rest of my life making it up to you, if you'll let me."

She felt the pinprick of tears.

"But it's your choice," Gage went on, that hint of vulnerability she'd seen earlier reappearing in his eyes. "I'll take you to the airport, let you go home to your family, and we never have to see each other again, if that's what you want."

"You can't be in l-love with m-me," she said in a choked voice.

The tears gathered as she took in the tender look on Gage's face.

"Why not?" he asked, his dimple appearing. "We're used to being two guarded people, but we let our guards down with each other."

"You can't..."

"What'll it take to convince you?" Gage joked, and then patted his clothes as if searching for something. "Maybe your Christmas gift?"

As Gage reached inside his pocket, Jacinda's eyes widened.

"I had something picked out for you," he said, "but I realized when you left the apartment that this was more appropriate."

"I don't have your gift! I—"

"Tossed it into the trash bin?" he finished for her, his tone droll.

"I left the tie at the apartment."

Gage smiled. "Just what I need. Another tie."

She blinked back her tears. "What do you recommend getting a billionaire?"

"I've got several suggestions about what you could give *this* billionaire that would make him very happy," he replied seductively.

She heated up at his suggestive tone.

Gage pulled out a jewelry case and flipped it open, and Jacinda felt her heart stop.

A round diamond in a beautiful latticework setting twinkled back at her.

"It's a family heirloom," Gage explained. "My ex-wife never wore it, because she was interested in something shiny and new. On the way here, I stopped by a jeweler who's a friend of mine and keeps a few things in his safe for me."

Emotion clogged her throat. "It's beautiful."

Gage took her hand. "Jacinda, will you marry me?"

"I haven't said I love you!"

"I'll take you on whatever terms I can get."

"Don't you ever stop?" she said, her laugh coming out as half a sob.

"Not when it's something I want badly. I love you, Jacinda."

Tears rolled down her cheeks. "Then aren't you lucky I'm in love with you, too!"

"Ah, sweetheart," Gage said, catching one of her tears with his thumb. "Don't cry."

"I can't seem to help it."

And in the next instant, Gage folded her into his arms and was kissing her senseless.

When they finally broke apart, Gage wiped at her tears, and she braced her hands on his chest.

"How will this work?" she asked, sudden worry tingeing her voice. "You live in New York, and I live in London."

"I've got a house in London," he replied. "We'll make it work if we want to."

She nodded, and then offered, "My firm has a New York office. I could always ask for a transfer."

"You'd do that for me?" Gage asked deeply.

"I'd like to keep my job, but I'm still willing to be your kept woman," she teased.

Gage groaned. "I'm going to have to work hard to live that one down."

Jacinda sobered a little. "I'll sign a prenup. I know your ex-wife—"

"I don't want a prenup with you," Gage interrupted. "Sweetheart, I'm willing to stay love-struck by you for the rest of my life."

Jacinda gave a watery laugh.

"Do you still want to head to the airport?" Gage asked, gazing into her eyes. "Because I'll understand if you want to spend Christmas with your family, especially since—"

Jacinda shook her head. "I called them and broke the news to them already."

She added more softly, "I want to spend the twenty-fifth with you, Gage. My family is already together and getting comfort from each other, but I can't think of a more comforting place for me to be right now than with you."

The look in his eyes warmed her heart.

"But I'd love it if you'd come to London with me soon to meet them."

He grasped her hand and raised it to his lips. "Of course. How does right after Christmas sound to you?"

"It sounds perfect."

After instructing the driver to turn the car around and head back to his apartment, Gage drew her to him. "Come here, and let me show you how to deliver an early Christmas gift I'd really appreciate."

Jacinda laughed, and then shot a glance at the front of the car. "Gage, we're not alone!"

"That's what the privacy partition and the tinted windows are for," he replied, dimpling.

And then they were too lost in each other to say anything more.

Epilogue

"What are you doing?" Gage asked, curious.

Jacinda stopped looking around them. "Taking notes."

He arched a brow. "On what?"

They were at Carrie and Trent Tanford's second wedding—a big, black-tie affair on New Year's Eve. After a church service, everyone had moved to a sit-down dinner at the Metropolitan Club, a two-story, white-marble space with a double staircase at one end and an enormous fireplace on the other.

Jacinda looked around where the two of them were sitting. "Wedding details. I want to get ours right."

Gage looked around, as well. Everything had been decorated with both a wedding and New Year's Eve theme in mind: silver, gold and white.

"Thinking of going with pink and gold for your own wedding?" he asked, unable to resist teasing her.

"Laugh if you want to," she responded, an expression of mock affront on her face.

Gage noted with satisfaction that, momentary teasing aside, Jacinda's expression lately had been all sunshine and light.

Once Kendrick had been arrested for Marie's death, Jacinda had acknowledged being ready to move on with her life in a way she hadn't been able to do for the past six months. And when her real identity had been revealed to the other residents of 721 Park Avenue, they had readily taken her into their inner circle, treating her as another victim of the crimes that had been perpetrated at their building.

For his part, Gage was glad Jacinda's future would include him.

"You know, I'm taking notes, too," he said, his eyes caressing her.

She looked surprised, happy. "On what?"

Leaning close, he whispered in her ear, "On how I'm going to get you out of that dress."

He grinned as he straightened, and she playfully slapped his arm.

His gaze raked over her.

She really did look terrific. Her claret V-neck satin dress was one he'd bought for her at Saks a couple of days ago, handing over his Amex Black Card with pleasure at money well-spent. The sleeveless dress showed off her shoulders and neckline to perfection.

Of course, he'd insisted on completing her look for the evening with a diamond-and-ruby necklace and earring set, which he'd surprised her with right before they'd departed for the wedding.

"What are you two lovebirds tweeting about?" Reed asked from the other side of the dinner table.

"The same thing you and your wife tweet about, Romeo," Gage retorted, getting a laugh from everyone around them.

Carrie and Trent had seated many of their fellow 721 Park Avenue residents at the same table.

"I doubt it," Reed shot back while Elizabeth, next to him, smiled. "Not unless you're talking about ways to relieve morning sickness, or teething pain in an eleven-month-old."

Gage had never seen Reed look more content. Parenthood seemed to agree with the Wellingtons. They'd been loving toward each other all evening, on one of their rare nights out without baby Lucus.

Still, Gage couldn't resist ribbing his neighbor. "A likely story. Tell it to the tooth fairy."

There was another round of laughter.

"Actually, Reed," Julia said, speaking up, "why don't you give a holler if you're up at two o'clock in the morning? Emma kept me and Max up last night until three."

Gage knew from photos he'd seen earlier in the evening that the Rollands had produced one cute baby.

"Ah, what we have to look forward to," Alex put in with a mock groan, squeezing Amanda's shoulder, his arm around the back of his fiancée's chair. "Makes me weak-kneed with gratitude that all Amanda and I are doing is planning a little bitty wedding."

"Can it, Alex," Reed responded good-naturedly. "We've been watching you dance attendance on Amanda all evening. When the time comes, you'll be pacing the floor with a howling bundle like the rest of us, and liking it."

"Busted," Amanda joked, but Alex just smiled easily.

"Speaking of weddings," Sebastian said, "Tessa and I hope you all will be attending ours in a couple of months in Caspia."

Jacinda clapped her hands. "I know Gage and I wouldn't miss it for the world. It's not every day we get invited to the wedding of an heir to the throne. I'll bet press from around the world will be there—"

"Stop," Tessa joked weakly, holding up a hand. "You're making me queasy just talking about it."

"Well, we can all do with some media attention of the upbeat variety, for a change," Gage put in.

The press had been all over Senator Kendrick's recent arrest.

"I'll second that," Trent Tanford agreed.

Gage turned his head and noticed the bride and groom approaching their table.

"Shouldn't you two be mingling with the guests?" Reed called.

"You are the guests," Trent shot back.

Carrie smiled as she stroked Trent's arm. "And anyway, we came to tell all of you there'll be a midnight dance in a few minutes to ring in the New Year."

"It's bound to be a good year for all of us," Gage

responded. "Vivian has put her apartment up for sale and is already living somewhere else."

"No kidding!" Sebastian and Trent said in unison.

Gage nodded in confirmation, knowing both Sebastian's and Trent's apartments were on the same floor as Vivian's, and guessing that the two men hadn't been looking forward to continuing as her closest neighbors. "The only reason Vivian isn't behind bars is that she cooperated with the police by offering up evidence against Senator Kendrick and implicating her lover, Henry Brown."

"What I want to know," Julia said, "is how and why. How did she do it?"

"Good question." Gage looked around the table. "Many of you probably don't know this, but Vivian's family used to own 721 Park Avenue. Though the family had to sell the property when their fortunes declined, they held onto ownership of one apartment—Vivian's. According to the police, Vivian's late husband used to be head of security for the building."

Reed's lips twisted. "So Vivian the ice queen had a track record of sleeping with the hired help."

Gage inclined his head, observing he had everyone's rapt attention. "I'll agree it's interesting. It also meant she was acquainted with security for the building."

Reed guffawed at the double meaning in Gage's words.

"So," Max said, finishing, "Vivian knew how to get access to everyone's apartments in order to use people's indiscretions against them."

"Exactly," Gage responded. "In fact, I think that's

why the SEC started investigating me and Reed for insider trading a couple of months ago. Vivian must have snuck into Reed's apartment or mine and misinterpreted, perhaps deliberately, some notes relating to a stock sale by the both of us. When Reed refused to pay blackmail money to keep his supposed financial misdeed hush-hush, Vivian retaliated by bringing the stock sale to the attention of the SEC."

Trent nodded. "It all makes sense. She and Henry must have sneaked into my apartment and found photos of me out with Marie. They must have copied the memory card on my digital camera and put it back before I discovered it was gone." He looked thoughtful. "When I refused to be blackmailed, they must have released the photos to the media."

"She or Henry must have gotten into all of our apartments," Max said in agreement. "That's how the blackmail schemes all started."

"But why?" Julia asked. "Why would she try to blackmail us?"

Gage grimaced. "The million-dollar question, if you don't mind another bad pun. According to the police, Vivian was pinched for cash after her husband's death. To support her lavish lifestyle, she took to blackmailing wealthy residents with Henry's help."

"To think I was afraid of her yapping dogs," Elizabeth Wellington said.

"Well, you won't have to worry about them any longer," Trent replied. "None of us will."

Jacinda was glad for that. Even so, she couldn't help letting her thoughts stray to what might have been.

"If Vivian hadn't been up to no good," she said sadly, "my sister might still be alive. Vivian's blackmail is what pushed Kendrick over the edge. He thought Marie was blackmailing him with a threat to make their relationship public. It looks as if he, like the rest of us, never suspected Vivian or Henry."

Elizabeth touched her arm sympathetically. "Jacinda, I'm so sorry. You've suffered even more than the rest of us in this whole episode."

There were murmurs of agreement around the table.

"Thank you," Jacinda replied, squeezing Elizabeth's hand. "Fortunately, I've gotten resolution now that Senator Kendrick is behind bars."

She looked around the table at all the faces offering sympathy and support. Her neighbors. Her new friends. "And I hope this will mean a new chapter in the life of 721 Park Avenue."

"Now that the rats among us have been eliminated, you mean?" Max asked rhetorically.

Jacinda smiled. "Not only that, but there's a parade of wedding bells and stork deliveries to look forward to."

She looked at Gage. He'd opened up and, these days, acted far from the guarded man she'd met six months ago.

She glanced back around the table. "For starters, Gage and I will be holding a regular open house at our apartment for Friday night TGIF drinks."

Gage raised his eyebrows, and then gave her a wink.

"Of course, the maid will be cleaning up before your arrival," she added teasingly.

Everyone laughed.

"I thought I recognized you when I bumped into you in the elevator," Sebastian put in.

"Sorry," she responded, "but I had to lie."

At Amanda's quizzical look, she explained, "Sebastian went to prep school in England with my brother. We hadn't seen each other in years, but when I ran into him in the elevator recently, he thought he recognized me. Of course, I had to convince him that I was Gage's maid so I could unearth the real story behind my sister's death."

"And you and Gage fell in love in the process," Tessa added with a grin. "How romantic. Like two spies falling for each other."

"Gage, you sly dog," Sebastian put in. "And here we all suspected you were just shagging the maid. It was even more complicated than that."

As Gage smiled enigmatically, Jacinda bit the inside of her mouth to keep from laughing.

No use telling everyone about how she had conned Gage, too, until recently, Jacinda thought. She was happy to let them think Gage had been in on her charade from the beginning.

After all, she'd gotten her hero.

However, she couldn't resist teasing by adopting an expression of pretend shock. "You all suspected Gage was shagging his housekeeper?"

Elizabeth laughed. "Yes, his disposition improved!"

"Yeah, we thought he must be getting some," Reed added with a sly grin.

Jacinda felt herself flush, but beside her, Gage laughed knowingly.

At that moment, the band began to play again, intruding on the conversation.

"I think that's our cue," Carrie said to Trent.

Amid a round of applause, Carrie and Trent walked over to cut the cake.

A short time later, after the cake cutting, Jacinda walked out onto the dance floor with Gage and the other couples of 721 Park Avenue to join the bride and groom and other guests for the midnight dance.

As the band began to play, all the couples swayed in a slow dance.

Gage's body pressed against hers, and Jacinda sighed, closing her eyes and resting her head on Gage's shoulder.

"Happy?" Gage murmured in her ear.

"Is it showing?" she whispered back, a smile curving her lips.

Gage laughed softly. "Only in the best way." He nuzzled her temple. "And speaking of showing, the baby boom in the building is giving me ideas."

She raised her head to look at him, even as her heart did a little flutter at his words.

She wanted to have a baby with Gage, she realized. He'd be such a good father. Attentive, loving. Everything he'd revealed himself to be already with her.

She tilted her head, and asked teasingly, "But aren't we getting married first?"

They'd agreed to have a May wedding in London, and then make 721 Park Avenue their home base. In fact, she'd already asked for a job transfer to the New York office of Winter & Baker.

Gage gave her a devilish look. "Yes, but we'll need to practice. Lots."

"Yes, please," she responded, and he laughed.

It was looking as if she'd be asking for another indefinite leave from Winter & Baker sooner rather than later.

Last week, after Christmas, she and Gage had flown to London and then on to Switzerland for a brief trip to break the news of their engagement to their parents.

Of course, both families had been delighted to hear of the engagement.

Jacinda reflected that her family in particular had welcomed the happy news at the end of a very difficult year. When she'd admitted she'd really been in New York sleuthing for the past six months, her parents had been taken aback and then belatedly concerned—even though she and Gage had spared them the details of how she'd masqueraded as his housekeeper without his knowledge. But even that wrinkle had soon been smoothed over, lost in the happiness over the engagement.

Now, as the last notes of the song faded away, the lead singer of the band took the mike.

Along with Gage and the other guests, Jacinda turned to look at the stage.

"It's the final seconds, folks," the singer announced. "Ten, nine…"

"Here it comes," Gage said in a low voice.

Everyone around them had started counting.

"…six, five…"

She looked up at Gage. "I'll love you just as much next year."

"Good to know," he replied, his dimple coming out. "…one…"

Gage's lips closed over hers as the crowd around them erupted with "Happy New Year!"

And there was no doubt in Jacinda's mind that this year *would* be a happy one for her and Gage. The first of many, she hoped.

They had a lot to look forward to—a wedding, children and a lifetime together.

They'd found each other.

* * * * *

Silhouette Desire kicks off 2009 with
MAN OF THE MONTH,
*a yearlong program featuring
incredible heroes by stellar authors.*

When navy SEAL Hunter Cabot returns home
for some much-needed R & R, he discovers he's
a married man. There's just one problem: he's
never met his "bride."

*Enjoy this sneak peek at Maureen Child's
AN OFFICER AND A MILLIONAIRE.
Available January 2009 from Silhouette Desire.*

One

Hunter Cabot, Navy SEAL, had a healing bullet wound in his side, thirty days' leave and, apparently, a wife he'd never met.

On the drive into his hometown of Springville, California, he stopped for gas at Charlie Evans's service station. That's where the trouble started.

"Hunter! Man, it's good to see you! Margie didn't tell us you were coming home."

"Margie?" Hunter leaned back against the front fender his black pickup truck and winced as his side gave a small twinge of pain. Silently then, he watched as the man he'd known since high school filled his tank.

Charlie grinned, shook his head and pumped gas. "Guess your wife was lookin' for a little 'alone' time with you, huh?"

"My—" Hunter couldn't even say the word. *Wife?* He didn't have a wife. "Look, Charlie..."

"Don't blame her, of course," his friend said with a wink as he finished up and put the gas cap back on. "You being gone all the time with the SEALs must be hard on the ol' love life."

He'd never had any complaints, Hunter thought, frowning at the man still talking a mile a minute. "What're you—"

"Bet Margie's anxious to see you. She told us all about that R & R trip you two took to Bali." Charlie's dark brown eyebrows lifted and wiggled.

"Charlie..."

"Hey, it's okay, you don't have to say a thing, man."

What the hell could he say? Hunter shook his head, paid for his gas and as he left, told himself Charlie was just losing it. Maybe the guy had been smelling gas fumes too long.

But as it turned out, it wasn't just Charlie. Stopped at a red light on Main Street, Hunter glanced out his window to smile at Mrs. Harker, his second-grade teacher who was now at least a hundred years old. In the middle of the crosswalk, the old lady stopped and shouted, "Hunter Cabot, you've got yourself a wonderful wife. I hope you appreciate her."

Scowling now, he only nodded at the old woman— the only teacher who'd ever scared the crap out of him. What the hell was going on here? Was everyone but him nuts?

His temper beginning to boil, he put up with a few

more comments about his "wife" on the drive through town before finally pulling into the wide, circular drive leading to the Cabot mansion. Hunter didn't have a clue what was going on, but he planned to get to the bottom of it. Fast.

He grabbed his duffel bag, stalked into the house and paid no attention to the housekeeper, who ran at him, fluttering both hands. "Mr. Hunter!"

"Sorry, Sophie," he called out over his shoulder as he took the stairs two at a time. "Need a shower, then we'll talk."

He marched down the long, carpeted hallway to the rooms that were always kept ready for him. In his suite, Hunter tossed the duffel down and stopped dead. The shower in his bathroom was running. His *wife?*

Anger and curiosity boiled in his gut, creating a churning mass that had him moving forward without even thinking about it. He opened the bathroom door to a wall of steam and the sound of a woman singing— off-key. Margie, no doubt.

Well, if she was his wife... Hunter walked across the room, yanked the shower door open and stared in at a curvy, naked, temptingly wet woman.

She whirled to face him, slapping her arms across her naked body while she gave a short, terrified scream.

Hunter smiled. "Hi, honey. I'm home."

* * * * *

Be sure to look for
AN OFFICER AND A MILLIONAIRE
by USA TODAY *bestselling author Maureen Child.*
Available January 2009 from Silhouette Desire.

CELEBRATE
60 YEARS
OF PURE READING PLEASURE
WITH HARLEQUIN®!

We'll be spotlighting a different series
every month throughout 2009
to celebrate our 60th anniversary.
Look for Silhouette Desire® in January!

Collect all 12 books in the Silhouette Desire®
Man of the Month continuity, starting in
January 2009 with *An Officer and a Millionaire*
by *USA TODAY* bestselling author
Maureen Child.

*Look for one new Man of the Month title
every month in 2009!*

www.eHarlequin.com   SDMOMBPA

SPECIAL EDITION™

**The Bravos meet the Jones Gang
as two of Christine Rimmer's famous
Special Edition families come together
in one very special book.**

THE STRANGER
AND TESSA JONES

by

CHRISTINE RIMMER

Snowed in with an amnesiac stranger during a
freak blizzard, Tessa Jones soon finds out her
guest is none other than heartbreaker Ash Bravo.
And that's when things really heat up....

*Available January 2009
wherever you buy books.*

Visit Silhouette Books at www.eHarlequin.com   SSE65427

Silhouette® Romantic SUSPENSE

**Sparked by Danger,
Fueled by Passion.**

Justine Davis

Baby's Watch

THE COLTONS
~FAMILY FIRST~

Former bad boy Ryder Colton has never felt a
connection to much, so he's shocked when he feels
one to the baby he helps deliver, and her mother.
Ana Morales doesn't quite trust this stranger, but
when her daughter is taken by a smuggling ring,
she teams up with him in the hope of rescuing her
baby. With nowhere to turn she has no choice but
to trust Ryder with her life...and her heart.

Available January 2009 wherever books are sold.

Look for the final installment of
the Coltons: Family First miniseries,
A Hero of Her Own by Carla Cassidy in February 2009.

Visit Silhouette Books at www.eHarlequin.com   SRS27614

REQUEST YOUR FREE BOOKS!

2 FREE NOVELS
PLUS 2
FREE GIFTS!

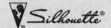

Passionate, Powerful, Provocative!

YES! Please send me 2 FREE Silhouette Desire® novels and my 2 FREE gifts (gifts are worth about $10). After receiving them, if I don't wish to receive any more books, I can return the shipping statement marked "cancel". If I don't cancel, I will receive 6 brand-new novels every month and be billed just $4.05 per book in the U.S. or $4.74 per book in Canada, plus 25¢ shipping and handling per book and applicable taxes, if any*. That's a savings of almost 15% off the cover price! I understand that accepting the 2 free books and gifts places me under no obligation to buy anything. I can always return a shipment and cancel at any time. Even if I never buy another book, the two free books and gifts are mine to keep forever. 225 SDN ERVX 326 SDN ERVM

Name	(PLEASE PRINT)	

Address		Apt. #

City	State/Prov.	Zip/Postal Code

Signature (if under 18, a parent or guardian must sign)

Mail to the Silhouette Reader Service:
IN U.S.A.: P.O. Box 1867, Buffalo, NY 14240-1867
IN CANADA: P.O. Box 609, Fort Erie, Ontario L2A 5X3

Not valid to current subscribers of Silhouette Desire books.

Want to try two free books from another line?
Call 1-800-873-8635 or visit www.morefreebooks.com.

* Terms and prices subject to change without notice. N.Y. residents add applicable sales tax. Canadian residents will be charged applicable provincial taxes and GST. Offer not valid in Quebec. This offer is limited to one order per household. All orders subject to approval. Credit or debit balances in a customer's account(s) may be offset by any other outstanding balance owed by or to the customer. Please allow 4 to 6 weeks for delivery. Offer available while quantities last.

Your Privacy: Silhouette Books is committed to protecting your privacy. Our Privacy Policy is available online at www.eHarlequin.com or upon request from the Reader Service. From time to time we make our lists of customers available to reputable third parties who may have a product or service of interest to you. If you would prefer we not share your name and address, please check here. ☐

SDES08F

® HARLEQUIN®

INTRIGUE®

KENNER COUNTY CRIME UNIT

Sabrina Hunter works hard as a police detective
and a single mom. She's confronted with her
past when a murder scene draws in both her
and her son's father, Patrick Martinez. But when
a creepy sensation of being watched turns into
deadly threats, she must learn to trust the man
she once loved.

SECRETS IN
FOUR CORNERS

BY

DEBRA WEBB

**Available January 2009
wherever you buy books.**

www.eHarlequin.com   HI69375

HARLEQUIN *Blaze*

UNIFORMLY HOT!

The Few. The Proud. The Sexy as Hell.

Four marines, four destinies, four complete short stories! While on a tour of duty, Eric, Matt, Eddie and Brian have become a family. Only now, on their way home from Iraq, they have no idea what—or *who*—awaits them....

Find out in

A FEW GOOD MEN

by

Tori Carrington.

Available January 2009
wherever you buy books.

**Look for one Uniformly Hot title
each month for all of 2009!**

www.eHarlequin.com   HB79449

You're invited to join our Tell Harlequin Reader Panel!

By joining our new reader panel you will:

- Receive Harlequin® books—they are FREE and yours to keep with no obligation to purchase anything!
- Participate in fun online surveys
- Exchange opinions and ideas with women just like you
- Have a say in our new book ideas and help us publish the best in women's fiction

In addition, you will have a chance to win great prizes and receive special gifts!
See Web site for details. Some conditions apply.
Space is limited.

To join, visit us at
www.TellHarlequin.com.

THBPA0108

Silhouette Desire

COMING NEXT MONTH

#1915 AN OFFICER AND A MILLIONAIRE—
Maureen Child

Man of the Month

A naval officer returns home to discover he's married…to a woman he's never even met!

#1916 BLACKMAILED INTO A FAKE ENGAGEMENT—
Leanne Banks

The Hudsons of Beverly Hills

It started as a PR diversion, but soon their pretend engagement leads to real passion. Could their Hollywood tabloid stunt actually turn into true love?

#1917 THE EXECUTIVE'S VALENTINE SEDUCTION—
Merline Lovelace

Holidays Abroad

Determined to atone for past sins, he would enter into a marriage of convenience and leave his new wife set for life. But a romantic Valentine's Day in Spain could change his plans….

#1918 MAN FROM STALLION COUNTRY—
Annette Broadrick

The Crenshaws of Texas

A forbidden passion throws a couple into the ultimate struggle—between life and love.

#1919 THE DUKE'S BOARDROOM AFFAIR—
Michelle Celmer

Royal Seductions

This charming, handsome duke had never met a woman he couldn't seduce—until now. Though his new assistant sees right through him, he's made it his business to get her into his bed!

#1920 THE TYCOON'S PREGNANT MISTRESS—
Maya Banks

The Anetakis Tycoons

Months after tossing his mistress out of his life, he discovers she has amnesia—and is pregnant with his child! Pretending they're engaged, he strives to gain her love *before* she remembers….

SDCNMBPA1208